HOME

HOME

KIMBERLY FULLER

TOR®

A TOM DOHERTY ASSOCIATES BOOK / NEW YORK

HOME

Copyright © 1997 by Kimberly Fuller

A Tor Book
Published by Tom Doherty Associates, Inc.
175 Fifth Avenue
New York, NY 10010

Tor Books on the World Wide Web:
http://www.tor.com

Tor® is a registered trademark of Tom Doherty Associates, Inc.

Design by Lynn Newmark

Library of Congress Cataloging-in-Publication Data

Fuller, Kimberly.
    Home/Kimberly Fuller.—1st ed.
        p. cm.
    ISBN 0-312-86152-4
    [1. Science fiction.] I. Title.
PZ7.F955456Ho   1997
[Fic]—dc20   96-41699
                                                  CIP
                                                   AC

First Edition: April 1997

Printed in the United States of America

0 9 8 7 6 5 4 3 2 1

To everyone I've ever known
And everyone I'll ever meet.
To Purrkins, my "Honey-Cat."
To my family, for giving me strength and courage.
And to Paul:
For the guidance
And the spirit, and everything else you have given me.
May you live a long and happy life.

ACKNOWLEDGMENTS

Home is actually one in a long line of efforts to write a book. I tried eight times before I finally hit on this story line. It worked. What a relief. I hope you enjoy it.

I have several people to thank. My parents and my brother, Randy, who know me better than most people and yet still tolerate me (ha-ha). All my friends: Tina, the B.F. since preschool; Heather-Bear, an excellent cook and medieval historian and one of my best friends in the world (It's your fault I wrote this, Bear! You and your books!); Shirley Mogg, for all the laughs and great times and for assuring me that everything I did, said, etc., was perfectly normal; Laila, for saying I'm one of her best friends, and always writing back; Jenny, for reading my odd bits and pieces, and for her friendship; "Ultraviolet" Geri, co-fan of The Greatest Rock Group in the World and an excellent and understanding person; Melanie, a beautiful girl and a great friend; Laurie, whose soul I know I've met somewhere before; the Haeberle family, for their company; Judy, whose beauty never ceases to amaze me; "West" Virginia for listening to my dreams and not telling; my pen pals worldwide for keeping me busy; Nancy, my soul sister and the first person I dared to let read the original manuscript; Michele, my wish-granter; Larry, for going the extra mile; Ned, for taking the time for me; Kris, for the great conversation and irreverence; my teachers, for their knowledge; Irv, for his care and common sense; Norm, for helping me through my hardest moments; Jay, who always takes a cookie for the road; and Bartley, for saving my life.

I would like to thank history, for its inspiration. The Roman slave revolt, Hannibal's defense of his homeland, the enslavement of Africans, the unjust treatment of Native Americans, the division of Ireland, and the Holocaust—all moved me greatly. This is for all those who know the meaning of the word "discrimination." May we learn from our mistakes.

Music is very important in my life so I also have to thank my "soundtrack" since most of this was written while listening to various types of music. Major portions were written to the tune of U2's *Achtung Baby* album, especially "One" and "The Fly," as well as *The Joshua Tree* album; Depeche Mode's *Songs of Faith and Devotion* album, especially "I Feel You," "Walking in My Shoes," and "Higher Love"; Peter Gabriel's *So* album. To those that know these songs and albums well: You will be able to hear the music in the background, I hope. To the people that are completely ignorant of all this music: Sorry.

Thank you all for your beautiful voices, moving lyrics, and great instrumentation. I couldn't have done it without you.

I

▲

THE
DISCOVERY

1

Touchdown. But where? His psyche stirred. He had landed, finally.

Finally.

After so many years of drifting, he had landed. The sensors had activated; they would tell him if it was safe—but that would take time.

He had waited this long.

He could wait a bit longer.

2

Did you see it?" Maran asked, lying down, her black mane of hair fanning out around her.

"See what?" Yandar Wix furrowed his brow. He crossed his legs, brushing the clinging sand from his knees.

"Something happened and no one told me?" Iri Makkaar looked up indignantly from where she sat, cross-legged, whittling on a piece of driftwood. Her dark complexion blended into the shadows of the cave.

"Do you mean the meteor?" Rheetah asked in her soft, lilting voice. Her crystalline blue eyes searched Maran's.

Daken Svenental's freckled face lit up with excitement. "You saw it too, Blondie?"

"Daken, don't call me that!" Rheetah snapped, glaring at him.

"Yes, the meteor." Maran rolled over onto her stomach. She grinned widely. "It was absolutely spectacular. Stunning. I don't ever recall seeing one brighter." She sat up, her hands moving excitedly as she spoke.

"I was walking outside, along the beach, and I looked out

across the ocean horizon and saw a brilliant red streak blazing through the sky. It was amazing!"

Daken picked up on Maran's story. "I was looking out my window. It must have been *huge*. It was so *bright*. At first I thought I was seeing things."

Rheetah gazed thoughtfully at Daken. "I wonder where it came down. Wouldn't it be thrilling to find it? What a treasure!"

Maran frowned. "A sunken treasure. From what I saw, I'd say it landed in the ocean. If that's the case, it's at the bottom by now."

"It's not fair that you saw it and I didn't." Iri sulked. She ran her blade over the smooth wood a few more times, then sheathed it.

"What if . . . What if it wasn't really a meteor? What if it was a visitor from outer space! Wouldn't that be something!"

"Daken, don't be stupid. It wasn't an alien spaceship." Iri looked at Daken Svenental as though she doubted his sanity. "Why would it land in the ocean? That's so dumb."

"No it isn't," Rheetah said, speaking up for Daken. "Maybe it crashed. Or maybe the aliens are aquatic people. That is possible."

Iri frowned again. "Not likely."

Maran rolled her eyes. "Stop bickering. I don't know what it was, but it was certainly beautiful. I'm thinking of painting a picture of it. What do you think?"

Rheetah nodded. "I can't wait to see it. It'll be great; you're a terrific painter. I can see it now—Captain Maran Thopel of Kalak Lar, the Second Colony of Terrat Du, Painter Extraordinaire."

Maran and the others laughed. "You give me too much glory, Rheet. I'm only in the fourth year of my command courses. I've got three more years to go before I'm even an ensign in the Space Corps, and much longer before I'm any sort of commander."

Rheet shrugged. "So? I've still got six more years of med school before I start rotations at the medical center. And Daken has four more years of mechanical engineering before he can even become an apprentice to one of the majors in the field.

Iri will finish before any of us since she's going for a degree in law enforcement and police science. But we wouldn't have been chosen for university unless we were the best of our classes, so I just *know* we'll make it big, and you'll make it the biggest of all, Maran."

"You think you've got it bad? A genetic engineer has to spend ten years getting educated and then three years in a specific program. I'll be dead before I can even get my own position at the university! I wish I could go into the program now. I already understand genetic makeup and how to mutate organisms. Put me on vegetable duty, I don't care, just get me out of school!"

Maran chuckled at her friend. "Wix, you're only seventeen, a year younger than Rheet and I. It won't take that long. You'll be there before you know it."

"I want to find the meteor." Iri ran her thumb over the smooth surface of her sculpture, a triangular arrangement of connected circles. "What do you think?"

"About the meteor or about your sculpture?" Maran cocked her head.

Iri shrugged. "Take your pick."

The group agreed that the sculpture was excellent, but the meteor intrigued them more.

"It could've landed on an island, I suppose," Maran said thoughtfully. "We could take a skiffer and check."

"Sounds great," Daken agreed. "What day?"

"How about . . . two days from now?" Maran spread her hands in question. They all agreed. "Great," she said. "In two days' time we get a skiffer and meet back here. The odds are against it, but maybe we'll get lucky and find the meteor after all."

3

Maran couldn't sleep. Each time her eyelids fell the image of the meteor's brilliant streak appeared in the darkness of her mind. She couldn't stop thinking about it. Suppose it really had landed on one of the atoll islands. It would be quite a find. She couldn't sleep for thinking. She needed to walk, to feel the sea breeze on her face and skin. She needed to get out of the house.

Maran rolled out of bed and shed her satin nightgown. She dressed in her black bathing suit, then pulled on her white shorts and lightweight white buttoned shirt. Stepping into her sandals, Maran cast a quick backward glance at her closed bedroom door and raised her windowpane. Then, as quietly as she could, she left her home and was out in the night.

She alighted softly on the ground, and with practiced feet she deftly stepped over her mother's flowers. Her mother's garden was beautiful, and destroying it in any way would give away her visits to the beach at nighttime, when all was silent and she could be alone. She threaded her way around the house perimeter to the street. Once there, she jogged to the south road that would take her out of town.

It was a mile hike to the beach; two-thirds on the road and one-third over the sandy plains. Most of the road was downhill, though, and the traveling would be easy. At least, it would be in one direction—coming back would be harder.

Maran passed the last of the city's houses and trotted along the road's edge. The light of the twin moons cast an eerie glow on the stone street, but Maran was glad to have the light around her. She would be able to see any animals or other travelers who might try to approach.

The road curved gently up ahead and Maran left its hard surface to walk on the beach grass that grew up from the shore. It was pale and short; the sand didn't provide much nutrition. It was for this very reason that the harvest fields were on the other side of the city, the side away from the shore. There the crops grew in the fertile soils of the hills, where the loose ground eroded from the mountains. The rich topsoil was full of nutrients so the corn and wheat flourished.

The site for the city had been chosen mainly because of the geography. It was a few miles from the mountains, so they wouldn't have to worry too much about flash floods and mudslides, but yet the city was up on a low hill, so they could look out and see the whole valley as well as the beach in the distance. To the west were the mountains, to the east was the beach. To the north were bogs, and then a thick forest that grew all the way up to the city. On the south side of the city, they had planted their crops as well as raised their livestock. The primary crops were a fibrous plant called *makkah* which was used in making fabrics, as well as *janolk*, a grain product used in breads. Furry "springer" beasts, much like deer, had been domesticated, and they fed placidly on the green and dark blue vegetation.

As she walked, Maran thought more of the meteor. She found herself considering many possibilities. As a command trainee, she was taught to keep an open mind about all situations. Someday, her teachers had said, this would help her make split-second decisions in battle. If she wasn't set in her ways, she could be flexible and outwit whatever enemies they might confront. An open mind was crucial for survival, they had taught her. Thoughts of Daken's suggestion suddenly found their way back into her mind.

The idea of alien spaceships was not outrageous. They themselves had come to Terrat Du from another world. It had been forty years since their landing; Maran was born twenty-two years after their arrival. Her father had died soon afterward. No one really knew the circumstances; he had disappeared while exploring the forest surrounding the village and never was found. But that was the past. The meteor, if that's what it was, *that* was the present. And the present was what concerned Maran.

She found herself entertaining wild fantasies of meeting strange three-armed creatures, being an ambassador of good-will to a new people. What would they be like? she wondered. It was impossible to know. She had frequently heard stories of little green men from space and had no reason to doubt them. But she had never even thought it possible to meet any aliens. *There aren't any aliens,* the logical part of her mind said. *It's a meteor, nothing more.* But the fantasy wouldn't leave her, and by the time she reached the bare sands of the beach, she could think of nothing else.

Maran made a quick detour to the cave where she and her friends would often meet and picnic when they came to the beach. It was in a cliff that was set near the beach, where a southern section of the mountains swung over and met the ocean. In the cave, Maran got her walking stick and stripped off her shorts. Then she went back outside to the ocean.

She kicked off her sandals and held them in her long fingers as she splashed leisurely through the still water. Unlike what she had heard of the origin planet, Terrat Du had fresh-water oceans. She bent down and scooped up a handful of water, taking a drink. She waded out up to her knees, using her stick to feel the way ahead of her steps. The atoll islands a mile out and the sandbars closer to shore prevented any breakers from hitting the beach. Only ripples played along the water-line.

The water tugged at her shirttails as Maran stood in the

knee-deep water. The moonlight on the water was beautiful.
She felt so at peace with herself when she stood in the ocean,
so in touch with her inner soul. On a whim, Maran unbuttoned
the front of her shirt and let the gentle breeze caress her skin.
She waded out up to her waist, the water warm and smooth
around her. It was the most wonderful feeling in the world, to
be alone like this. Alone with nature.

She looked down at her reflection in the moonlight. Even
though she had never seen her father, Maran knew she looked
like him. Where her mother was a blue-eyed, well-tanned
blonde, Maran was fair complexioned, with thick black hair that
she let flow past her shoulders. It was her eyes that drew the
most attention—they were violet, a dark, dusky purple that no
one else in the colony possessed. Maran had searched through
all her family records trying to find anyone who matched her
physical appearance, but she was unsuccessful. Often she wondered how she came to look as she did, but sometimes she
rather enjoyed being unique among her people and knew she
would not trade her appearance.

Maran looked out over the water at the largest atoll island.
Is it out there? she wondered to herself. Would it be waiting for
them, the meteor? Or would something else be waiting, something foreign and exotic, unlike anything they had ever seen?
Unlike anything they had ever even imagined?

She turned and began to move down the shore. The water
opposed her movements and she could feel the muscles in her
legs working. She plunged the walking stick ahead of her feet,
stirring the water to frighten away any bottom dwellers. The
last thing she needed was to step on a poison-tailed *thillu'gat*
when she wasn't even supposed to be out of her home.

Maran was gazing absently at the water when she suddenly
noticed something riding low in the ripples several yards from
the shore. She trudged up to the sand and higher ground to
get a better view. It was a black capsular object, about six feet
long, bobbing in the gentle tide. Electrified, Maran threw off
her shirt and quickly waded out into the ocean and to the capsule. She thrashed the water with her stick and finally reached

the object. Treading water, she swam it back to the shore and beached it.

Her hair wet and her body glistening in the moonlight, Maran studied the object. It was unlike anything she had ever seen. It was completely black and smooth, seamless. On one side was a short row of colored lights. They were buttons of some sort, she decided. One of them must open the capsule. At this thought, a thrill ran through her body. What could be inside it?

Maran's fingers hovered hesitantly over the colored buttons. Should she open it now, or get the others? It would be a long, uphill walk back. But what if whatever was inside was dangerous? She could die out here, alone, with this *thing* unleashed on Terrat Du. No, she would have to get the others. If she ran, she could make good time.

Maran slipped on her sandals and scooped up her shirt. Leaving her walking stick on the beach, she ran back up the slope to the plain. Her feet pounded against the sandy soil, her white shirt flapping open in the wind she caused. Her breath came hard and she started to feel dizzy even as she reached the road, but still she didn't slow her pace. By the time she was back inside the city limits of Kalak Lar, her town, Maran was thoroughly winded from going up the gentle hill. To avoid undue suspicion, she slowed her pace to a leisurely trot.

First she would get Iri. Then Rheet. But what to tell them? *I found it! I found it!*

Maran ran around the side of Iri's house to her window. She stepped through the flower bed and rapped on the pane, standing on her tiptoes.

"Iri! Iri, wake up! Wake up, I found it!"

Iri came to the window and raised the pane, leaning her forehead against the screen. Her short hair was mussed, her face still cloudy with sleep.

"What do you want? Found what?" She rubbed her dark eyes.

"Daken was right! I found it! It washed up on the beach. Iri, come with me, we have to open it. We have to open it!" Maran was breathless with excitement.

Iri shook her head and rubbed the back of her neck. She stared at Maran for a moment, thinking, before speaking. "Lemme get dressed. I'll be out in a minute."

"While you do that, I'll go wake Rheet. I'll be right back." Maran dashed across the street.

4

The five friends slid down the slope to the beach. The capsule rested in the surf near Maran's walking stick. It glistened black and mysterious in the light of the twin moons, darkly beckoning to them. They approached it cautiously.

Rheet slung her backpack off her shoulder. She took out her med scanner and held it up, focusing on the sleek object.

"I'm getting readings . . . Something . . . Something's alive in there." The statement was whispered, reverently.

Wix crouched beside Rheet, his eyes riveted to the pod. "It's beautiful," he breathed. "I've never seen anything like it in my life. Never."

Iri slowly drew her stun gun. "None of us have, Daken. We've got to take this slowly, very slowly. And very, very carefully. One wrong move and we could all be dead."

Rheet nodded. "Iri's right. Daken, did you bring the shield like I asked?"

"Got it," Daken replied. He took four rods out of a sack, held them out to her. Rheet took them and pounded them into the ground in a square formation around the pod. Then, one by one, she switched them on. A low hum followed, and the rods glowed green.

"Quarantine field established. Now what?" Rheet looked up at Maran.

Maran was staring at the quarantine rods. "Where did you get those?" she asked.

Daken shrugged, shuffling his foot in the sand. "Well, I *am* a top engineering student, and that *does* give me priority access . . ."

Maran rolled her eyes. "So you stole them. Is that it?"

Daken sighed. "*Steal* is such a bad word. I prefer *borrow*. And, no, I didn't steal or borrow them. I was working on a project for class and they were out on loan to me. Nothing more."

Iri sighed loudly. "Can we get on with this? Dawn isn't that far off and it looks like a storm might blow in tonight."

Maran nodded. She ran her hand over the surface of the pod. "Someone is going to have to open it. And someone will have to greet . . . whatever is inside it. I found the pod; I volunteer." She looked up at her friends to gauge their reaction.

At first, they were all silent. Then Rheet spoke.

"I hate to admit it, but Maran's right. The rest of us will stand outside the field, just beyond the perimeter. Iri, be ready with your stunner. If it makes any hostile move, blast it. Don't wait. Daken, take special note of how the pod operates. You may want to record it with your scanner. I'll be standing next to Iri, monitoring the . . . being's . . . vital signs at all times. Maran, as soon as that thing opens, step back. I'll do a level-three microorganism scan to filter out any diseases that it might bring. The last thing I want is to drop the field and let some deadly sickness escape. As soon as we've determined it's safe, the field goes down." She took a deep breath, tucked a lock of blond hair behind her ear. "Are we ready?"

The group nodded.

Rheet adjusted her med scanner. "Then let's do it. Positions, everyone."

The five took their places, Maran within the field, her hands resting lightly on the pod's sleek metal surface. Her fingers hovered over the buttons; she was guessing at which one to press and hoped it didn't end up destroying whatever was inside it. Out of the corner of her eye, she saw Rheet nod, giving the signal. Hesitantly, Maran chose a button. She laid her fingers against its surface—and pressed it.

The pod was silent. Maran held her breath, stepped backward a pace. Then it began to hum, a deep rumble that vibrated even the air. A crack appeared in the top of the pod and began to widen as they watched. A red light pulsed from within and suddenly a burst of steam spewed from the object. Startled, Maran threw up her hands, but she was wrapped in the cloud and concealed from view.

"Maran!" Iri yelled, raising her blaster. But Rheet caught her wrist.

"No, Iri! It's all right." Rheet raised her med scanner and initiated a level-three probe. "Scanning starts now. Level three . . . Clean . . . Level two . . . Clean . . . Level one . . . Clean. It's safe. From what I can tell."

The fog continued to pour out of the black object, forming a thick cloud, traveling along the sand and wrapping around itself, the pod, and Maran. The hum grew louder and the crack continued to widen as the sides began to slide down underneath the pod itself. Finally, after many minutes, the hum subsided and the fog dissipated.

Maran stood with her back to Rheet and Iri, staring at the being within the pod. Her breath caught in her throat and her eyes widened.

A male lay inside. He was dressed completely in black and wore black boots. There was a strange insignia on the left breast of his jacket. He had fair skin that was lightly freckled, and hair that was thick and black, swept back from his forehead and down to the nape of his neck. Maran observed his somewhat high forehead, his dark eyebrows, high cheekbones, and his jawline, where black stubble lightly grew, then across his chin.

He bore a striking resemblance to Maran's people. She imagined him grinning at her, and smiled in spite of herself. *He's amazing*, Maran thought to herself, the one coherent thought she had managed since she first saw him. Iri's voice jarred her out of her reverie.

"Maran, are you all right? How are you feeling?"

Maran pulled herself back to the real world. She felt slightly dizzy and told Iri as much. Rheet scanned her but found no abnormal results.

"Maybe you're just shocked from the discovery. I know I am," Rheet said softly.

Iri impatiently shifted her stunner from hand to hand. "Well, since it's safe, how about we go take a closer look?" Rheet turned off the quarantine field and the four surged forward as one.

Iri approached cautiously, her stunner at the ready. Rheet kept her eyes on her med scanner the whole time, reading off the report as it appeared.

"Subject is male, bipedal, high brain development, with basic organs very similar to ours. Body temperature approximately ninety-six and rising, blood pressure sixty over forty-five and rising steadily—approaching normal, whatever that is—heart rate is fifty-four and rising steadily. I'd say he's recovering quickly from the stasis hibernation. He appears to be in perfect health." She stood over him opposite Maran. "Now, will he speak? That's what I want to know."

Maran nodded, though she barely heard her friend. She couldn't take her eyes off this man's face. Of all the aliens she had imagined finding, never had she dreamed it would look like this. She had braced herself for something green and slimy, or something furry with seven arms and three heads. But not this. Not this at all.

Daken was examining the pod itself, taking measurements and readings and entering them in his scanner. He frowned and scratched his head.

"What's up, Daken?" Iri asked, stunner still on the alien.

"This metal that the pod is constructed from—it's native to this planet, our Terrat Du. Now I suppose that it could also be found any number of other places in the universe, but it's a remarkable coincidence. And the life-support systems—they withdrew the moment the crack in the hull appeared. It must be some kind of automatic response, but I certainly wouldn't call it safe. What if the pod landed on an asteroid or a hostile planet? If it opened . . ."

"Daken, don't hypothesize, just tell us the facts," Iri said impatiently.

"Okay, okay," Daken replied. He glared at Iri. "As I was saying, the fact that it did open must have had something to do with Maran's pushing of the button. I can't imagine what would've happened if no one had been here. Would it have opened? I don't know. I'll have to do further studies. But I do know that it's amazing he's in such perfect physical condition."

"Why do you say that, Daken?" Wix asked.

"Because from the wear on the hull's exterior and the atmospheric readings inside the pod, I'd say he's been in here about . . . twenty years or so—give or take a few, of course."

Rheet looked down at her scanner. "Biologically, I can't tell how old he is. The stasis has stopped him from physically aging, as well as stopping anything that would be telltale, like loss of bone material or cellular degeneration. However, he does not appear to be much older than any of us. His temperature and blood pressure have stabilized at what I would call normal. I'd say he's through the worst of it. But you're right, Daken. I'm amazed, too. No muscle atrophy, no cellular breakdown—this is one highly sophisticated stasis system we're dealing with, folks. I'm impressed. Even our systems aren't that good. They require months of physical therapy to restore muscle tone, even after less than a year in stasis. This is truly incredible."

The man's lips parted, but only Maran saw. "Shhh! He's waking. Quiet!" Maran leaned over him, cocking her head slightly to listen. The others tensed in anticipation. Rheet and Daken adjusted their scanners nervously while Iri took aim with her stunner. She knew that at this close range, she had to be able to move faster than he could. They waited anxiously for something to happen.

The man drew a long breath as his tongue lightly wet his lips. His lashes fluttered experimentally, then his eyes opened.

They darted about, taking in his surroundings, then focused on
Maran's face, his eyes meeting hers. Maran gasped as the moonlight danced in their depths.

"My gods . . . ," she whispered.

His eyes were violet.

The man continued to stare raptly at Maran, his strange violet
eyes unblinking. His lips parted again, and he uttered a single
word: ". . . De . . .?"

His voice was soft and slightly husky. It harbored a slight
accent that Maran could not identify, but she found its timbre
very pleasant. She looked at him a moment, stunned, then with
careful enunciation, she answered.

"My name is Maran Thopel. What is your name?" she asked
him.

He paused a moment, as though fetching the memory from
deep within himself. His brow furrowed in thought and his eyes
briefly closed. "Aliksandar, *un drek la* Pellen."

Maran smiled, wondering if he could understand her language, since he had spoken in a strange tongue. Behind her,
the others murmured quietly. "Aliksandar," Maran said, "as
representatives of the race of people known as the Frathi, we
welcome you to the planet we call Terrat Du."

Aliksandar looked up at the sky. He squinted hard, his eyes
searching the heavens, taking note of the moons and the star
positions. For a long moment he was silent as the moonlight
reflected on his face and in his eyes. He seemed to be searching in his mind for something he had lost. "Frathi?" he whispered carefully. "Terrat Du? No. This is Arakka. Arakka." He
paused, and Maran hid her surprise that he had spoken in her
language. The strange man returned his gaze to Maran. "I
have come home."

5

A light drizzle had begun to fall and the six people huddled in the meeting cave. Alik had been wrapped in an
opened-out sleeping bag. The sleeping bags were left at the cave
in case a situation like this ever arose and they needed—or
wanted—to stay in the cave overnight. An electric lantern cast
its flickering light from the cave's center. The battery was low
and Daken had forgotten to bring a new one. But the unsteady
glow wasn't noticed as the group listened to Alik relate the story
of his journey.

"Forty years ago, my people had been invaded by beings
from another world. We the Arakkans had a fairly high tech-
nology level, but we were peaceful and had few weapons to defend ourselves. We were quickly defeated and driven from our
homes to live in refugee camps in the forest and the mountains.
While in refuge, we built a spaceship and sent out explorers that
would hopefully find a new world. Seventy men and women
were put in stasis pods and loaded onto a transport ship. If anything happened to the ship, the pods were to be ejected and a
tracking signal would guide them home. If the pods were for-

tunate enough to land, the colonists would start a new life."

"But who would open the pods? If Maran hadn't opened yours, you would still be inside that thing. Wouldn't you?" Iri raised an eyebrow at Alik skeptically.

"Actually, once I landed, the sensors on the pod were activated to take atmospheric readings. After twenty-four hours if everything was safe, the pod would've opened itself. But it is also equipped with a manual system for opening." He looked pointedly at Maran. "The only catch is trusting the person that opened the pod. If an enemy had opened the pod, I could have been killed in the few seconds before my regaining full consciousness."

Maran had been attentively listening to what Alik was saying. Her eyes wouldn't leave him. Even though she had known him less than an hour, Maran already had memorized every aspect of his face. She was intrigued by him, of this there was no doubt. *Is it because he's an alien, is that why I'm so curious about him?* Maran wondered to herself. She longed to talk with him alone, to find out what he was really like. He seemed so like her. And his eyes . . . It was unnerving the way they seemed to bore into her very soul.

"How old are you, Alik?" Rheet asked.

"When the Shlatlar came, I had seen twenty-two cycles. The Shlatlar called them years, I remember. The pod slowed my aging, though. So I am still not much older than that. But I do not know how old I am."

Rheetah nodded. "I had suspected that your aging had been slowed, since I couldn't get an accurate reading."

Wix looked over his shoulder at the sky outside the cave. "It's getting worse out there. We should be heading home if we're going to beat the storm." The others nodded in agreement and Maran snapped back to reality. Alik's eyes followed her as she rose from her seat on the floor and dusted the sand off her legs. Rheet and Daken gathered up their equipment and replaced it in the backpack. Iri helped Maran drag out and open up two other sleeping bags to make a pallet for Alik. Daken brought out part of their food cache that they stored in a rear chamber.

"You can eat this if you get hungry," he explained. "There's more back there, if you need it."

Alik smiled. "Thank you," he replied.

Daken shrugged. "No problem. You *are* new here. That's what friends are for."

Alik nodded slowly. "Yes, friends." He turned to Maran, looking into her eyes. "Maran, we are . . . friends?" In his tone, Maran could distinctly hear him wonder if she would betray him.

Maran's heart raced. The alien, the man from another world, wanted to be her *friend.* "Alik, I would be honored to be considered your friend."

Alik grinned and offered his hand to her. She took it, and he grasped her hand firmly but gently. Maran felt herself flush. His hands were so strong, but he was so careful not to hurt her. And they were so soft. She would never have guessed their softness. She only reluctantly let go of him. He turned with Daken and retreated into the back of the cave.

Iri sheltered her eyes and peered out into the grumbling darkness. "We need to be going. Come on, guys, get a move on."

Rheet and Wix shouldered the bags. Daken reemerged, finished spreading out Alik's bed, and then stood. "I'm ready. How about you, Maran?"

Maran dragged her attention away from the chamber where Alik had disappeared. "Um . . . Iri?" Iri turned around to face her friend and raised her eyebrows. "Iri, I'd like to stay here tonight. Mother is leaving for Kalak Singh early in the morning; she won't check on me first, I know. She won't realize that I'm gone."

Iri stared levelly at Maran, motioning her over and drawing her aside. "Maran, what are you doing, hmmm? What's up your sleeve? Does you have an ulterior motive?" She looked meaningfully at Maran.

Maran was a bit shocked at her friend's remark. "Iri! How could you even suggest such a thing? I merely want to use this time to get to know our alien friend, to find out about his culture, his people. That's all."

Iri frowned doubtfully. "Uh huh. I bet. Look, as long as you won't get in trouble with your mom, I don't care if you stay. But keep the stunner," Iri said, pressing the weapon into Maran's hand, "you never can tell what might happen." Maran nodded in reply.

"Thanks, Iri. I appreciate your concern. I'll keep it." She tucked the blaster into the back pocket of her shorts. Iri frowned again, eyeing Maran's clothes, but decided to let it pass. Instead, she turned to the others and told them the plan.

"You're staying?" Rheet asked softly. "Are you sure?"

Maran nodded and patted the stunner. "I'll be okay," she assured her friend. Rheet nodded in return and, with the others, stepped out into the rainy night. Maran was left alone with Alik.

She sighed and unrolled another sleeping bag. *What a day!* She tucked the blaster under its edge and sat down just as Alik emerged from one of the back chambers of the cave. He had changed from his other clothes into a pair of Wix's black shorts. The sight of his bare legs and chest made Maran's cheeks flush against her will. She hastily looked down at her hands as he sat down across from her on his makeshift bed, crossing his legs. He looked around the cave, frowning.

"Where are the others?"

Maran cleared her throat, unsure of how to answer. "They went home. The weather is getting worse. I wanted to stay."

He gazed at her intently. "Why?"

Maran blinked. "Why what?"

"Why did you want to stay?" He took a bite out of a piece of fruit and chewed slowly.

Maran suddenly found herself unable to speak. Why, again, had she wanted to stay? "I . . . I wanted to talk to you. To find out about you. You know, um, what your home world is— was—like. Is that all right?"

Mischief danced in his eyes. "If you want to stay, I would find that . . . not disagreeable."

Maran blushed. Trying to distract herself, she picked up her recorder and ran her thumb over its sleek surface. "Do you mind if I tape this . . . interview?"

He smiled, looking at her through his thick black lashes. "If that will please you."

Maran cleared her throat. "Oh." She switched the recorder on. "First, is there anything you *don't* want to talk about?" He leaned forward on his elbow. "Whatever you want to talk about, I will. I am open to anything." His voice was soft, almost a whisper.

"Okay then. Let's see . . . where to start . . . Tell me about your people. Tell me what happened when you were invaded. What did they do?"

He ran his hand over his hair. To Maran, he seemed to be searching for all the correct words and putting them together in the right formats before he spoke. "To tell the story," he said at last, his Frathi still a bit slow and unsteady, "you must know about our minds. We the Arakkans believe in one god, called Tahar. He created the World and planted the Seeds that grew the People. They took many years to germinate and grow. Civilization spread over the surface of Arakka but we never forgot the Founder, the One Who Started Everything. We built temples, monuments, worshipping centers—all in his honor. We believed that when we died we journeyed to the Cloud to live with him. We believed he protected us every moment of our lives and that we should trust him at all times." Alik stared past her at the wall for a moment before continuing.

"I remember when the invaders came. We called them the Shlatlar—the Destroyers. They burned our homes and our schools. They massacred our animals and ravaged our crops. We ran to the worship centers, knowing that Tahar would protect us and the Shlatlar wouldn't dare attack us there. But they did." He closed his eyes. "They did. I remember the screams of the women and children, the valiant fighting of the men as the Shlatlar broke through the doors, guns spewing death and destruction. I remember the beautiful colored windows shattering as the people fought to escape and were cut down in their flight. It seemed hopeless; they were so powerful and we, being a peaceful people, had few ways to defend ourselves. We prayed to Tahar to save us, to take away the Shlatlar. The priestesses and priests fasted and performed ritual chants. But still, death continued to litter the streets, and the men marched off to a futile battle." He sighed and shook his head.

"It was all so senseless. The fighting, the blood, it was just so senseless. They didn't understand us. We would have gladly shared our world with them. Tahar told one of the ancient priests: 'Share your home and you will receive a greater one. Give of yourself and you will have everything you need.' But the Shlatlar wanted it all for themselves. During all this time of the battle, our population had been reduced from five billion to less than a million. Many of our continents were sunk when the Shlatlar ship fired on oceanic rifts and edges of tectonic plates. Many were simply killed in aerial bombing attacks."

He paused for a moment to collect more words, and Maran took the opportunity to ask him a question: "How did any of you ever survive the air raids? Certainly those ships could have completely wiped out the Arakkan society."

He nodded and continued. "The heavy warfare drained the Shlatlar ship's weapon supplies, and they were forced to land because they didn't have the materials to replenish their fuel and weapons. But even in a land battle, the odds weren't much more even, although a team of Arakkan men did manage to infiltrate the ship and irreparably burn out the computer system. This brought only more retribution onto us, but at least it didn't come from the sky.

"Finally, an answer came. Tahar answered our prayers. The Umak'Daahl'Sleur, the highest of the high priests, had gone into the forest to one of the remote temples to fast. It was there that Tahar created a vision for the Umak to see, a vision of a great black ship into which the People swarmed. It sailed through the stars to another land where the People lived their lives in harmony. He went back to the city and told the First of the High Council of his vision; the First commanded construction of the great ship to begin immediately. The Umak'Daahl'Sleur designed the plans and managed the building of the ship and its interior pods. It was built over two years deep within an underground chamber. Then those who would be taken on the ship were called in secret.

"Only men and women between the ages of twenty and

forty-five were allowed to go. I was one of the first. I can still vividly recall being attached to the life support and feeling my world grow dim around me as the pod was sealed. The pods were really only a fail-safe in case something happened to the ship; then the pods hopefully would find their way back home with a long-distance beacon. Apparently, something did happen to the ship, or I wouldn't be here now."

"Is there a master plan? What do you do now that you're back?"

He paused a moment. "Well, initially the Umak had hoped that one of our own would open the pod. But that hasn't happened." He hesitated. "In the case that an Arakkan did not find the Returned, then we were to seek out our own and reunite with them. But I have no idea where to begin, really. I am on Arakka, but I may be the last of our kind. And if I *am* the last, then there is nothing at all I can do."

"So . . . What makes you say that this was your home-world?"

Alik finished off the fruit. "The stars. When I was a boy, my grandfather taught me all the constellations and where they would be each season. I have always loved the stars and I've kept track of them all my life. This *is* Arakka, I would stake my soul on it."

Maran nodded awkwardly. She felt very odd about being alone in this cave with someone who was claiming her world to be his own. She didn't know how to react to his statements. Should she agree? Should she disagree? Her mind sat in a state of confusion. "I'm glad you told me your story," she finally said.

"Thank you," he replied, leaning back against the cave wall.

And what about my safety? she thought to herself. Would he try to hurt her because her people had supposedly taken his world? Had she risked her life by staying?

I shouldn't be here. This is too dangerous. I should've waited to talk to him with Iri and the others. She cut off the tape, then stood and turned to look out the cave mouth. Rain poured from the dark sky. Though she would become drenched and it would be a rough walk, she could make it home. But should she leave?

Suddenly, Maran felt Alik's hands resting lightly on her shoulders. Her body stiffened and her breath caught in her throat. She wished the stunner was with her and not under the sleeping bag.

"Maran," he whispered, his voice barely audible over the rain, "I am glad you have stayed. I would not want to spend my first night here, alone, with this storm. Though I know Tahar is always with me, your being here has brought me great comfort. I thank you for your generosity."

Maran forced herself to swallow. "I'm happy to stay, Alik. Whatever I can do for you, let me know." *I think. Just don't ask me to kill anyone or try to singlehandedly get your planet back.*

Alik turned her around to face him, taking her hands in his and slowly sitting down in the sand, bringing her with him.

"Maran," he whispered, still holding her hands, "why are you so nervous? Am I that threatening?" His eyes gazed into hers.

"I'm . . . not . . . nervous . . . It's just . . . I'm not used to . . ." Her voice trailed off as she stumbled over the words. How could she explain that what she felt wasn't true fear but something else, something she couldn't even name. It wasn't fear, it was anticipation. Maran knew that something was going to happen. She wasn't sure of its nature, but something would happen to her because of him and it would change her life. She didn't want her life changed—the very thought of it made her head throb, her chest ache, her muscles stiff. It made her breathing tight and her pulse race in her palms. Palms that Alik still gently held.

He was smiling softly at her, his violet eyes kind. "Maran, you can't imagine what it was like for me, waking up and seeing you. I knew that I must be dead and at the Cloud and that you were one of Tahar's servants. But when I realized that I was alive and you"—he paused—"you were alive, too, I was overwhelmed. After all these years, to come home and find . . ." He broke off as his voice caught. He paused, looking down at Maran's long, delicate fingers, then back up to her eyes. "There was a prophecy, a message given to the Travelers before we left the origin world. 'Whoever opens the eyes of the First to Return will lead his people to a new frontier.' " His gaze intensified. "You are that person, Maran."

Maran's eyes widened. "No! I can't be . . . I'm not . . . I'm just a . . . a . . ."

"I don't know where the other pods are. Perhaps they were lost. I know they haven't landed, because my pod would have told me through the pad under my ear. It would have said "Third" or "Fifth" or "Seventieth." But it said "First." And even though the pod would have opened automatically, I feel that I owe everything to you because you had the courage to release me and you have helped me in these first few hours when I've been of less strength. You gave me food and fresh water. You have kept me company. I feel I almost owe my life to you." He held her eyes in his gaze again before bowing his head to kiss her hand. His lips rested briefly against her skin and Maran felt color rise in her cheeks. His lips were so soft, so gentle—*I wish he would kiss me,* the irrational part of her said, but it was quickly stifled. Her eyes met his as he looked back up at her.

His eyes seemed to draw her in, to drown her in emotion. The irrational part of her returned full force as he softly cupped her jaw in his hand. He slowly cocked his head, as though trying to understand why she blushed so, why her breath shook in her throat like it did. Then he began to lean toward her, his eyes fluttering shut as he slowly closed the distance between them.

Maran shut her eyes in anticipation. *Oh gods of the cloud, he's going to kiss me!* The thought slammed through her brain. She could feel his breath soft and warm on her face. *Oh gods, oh gods . . .* The aroma from the fruit he had eaten wrapped around them, cloaking them in its sweetness as the dark clouds cloaked the twin moons. A gust of wind blew into the cave, toppling the lantern, and the cave was plunged into darkness as his lips ever so softly brushed against her cheek. The kiss, if that was what it could be called, was brief, but to Maran it lasted an amazing eternity. She felt her heart skip in her chest and her nerves tingle as he ran his hands down her shoulders and released her.

Maran opened her eyes only to discover that she couldn't
see. But even that took a few moments to register in her hazy,
whirling mind. "The lantern," she finally whispered. After convincing her muscles to move from their position, she crawled
over to where she remembered it standing and reactivated it.
Alik was still seated on the sandy cave floor, watching her. He
smiled slightly.

Maran cleared her throat, holding the lantern in her hand.
"I need to be getting to sleep." She edged over to her sleeping bag, opened it, and climbed into the pallet. "You should
do the same."

Alik nodded, eyes twinkling in the dim light. He smoothed
his makeshift bed, then climbed in, pulling up the covers
around his waist. He turned on his side and propped himself
up on his elbow, still looking at Maran. Trying not to notice,
Maran leaned over and turned down the light to its dimmest,
placing it in the sand between them. She looked over at Alik in
time to see him smiling impishly at her. Maran blushed deeply
and turned away. "Good night, Maran," he whispered, sliding
down off his elbow and folding his arms under his head. "Pleasant dreams."

"Good night, Alik." Maran replied, closing her eyes. The
image of his grin lingered, floating like a phantom in her mind.
She was exhausted from running back and forth from the beach
to Kalak Lar. From the excitement of discovering the pod.
From meeting Aliksandar Pellen. *Alik . . . Alik Pellen . . . Aliksandar . . . Aliksandar Pellen . . .* His name danced through her
head. Maran smiled to herself as the waves of sleep pulled her
down and claimed her.

6

Maran awoke just before dawn. She went through some of the clothes that were kept at the back of the cave and pulled on a better shirt and a pair of shorts. Aliksandar was still sleeping soundly and she did not wish to disturb him. Silently, she went outside to watch the sun rise. Unlike the others, Maran didn't have classes today. She planned to spend her time with Alik.

Normally, she had classes three times a week. She would often meet two or more of her friends for lunch in the midafternoon, and then after two more classes they would all walk home together. Sometimes they would visit the beach in the evening, or they would spend time together at someone's house. Generally, if they had that in mind, they would go to Rheetah's house. She would always cook them something and they would eat and talk. Maran knew she would be missing out on time with her friends, but this was important to her.

The sky had already begun to wax pink as the sun initiated its daily crawl upward. Maran sat down in the sand, her toes tickled by the ripples of the ocean, and watched the sun rise. It seemed to stare at her like a great eye as she watched it in return.

"It's been a long time since I've seen a sunrise." The voice startled Maran and she jumped, turning quickly around.

"Alik! Good morning. How did you sleep?"

He sat down in the sand beside her, stretching his legs into the water. "I slept well, thank you." He smiled, feeling the water caress his skin. The orange glow of the rising sun danced on the ripples. "I had a strange dream, though. Knives. There were many knives. And guns. And there was a podium of sorts." He paused. "You were standing at it, speaking." He looked over at her. "You were very emphatic about whatever it was that you were saying. I remember being impressed."

Maran frowned, considering his dream, rolling it over in her mind. "I studied dream analysis. Let me see if I can figure out what that means." She paused, thinking. "Well, guns and knives could be symbols of impressing your opinion on someone. And my speaking at a podium . . . that would be like making a speech for or against something. Maybe it's about a rally, or something to that effect, or about you trying to convince yourself or someone else to do or think a certain thing. What do you think?"

Alik nodded slowly. "There were many people. Yes, it could've been a rally of some kind . . ." He paused and studied the eddies of water around his toes before continuing. "Now all I have to do is wait for it to come true."

Maran glanced sharply at him. "What do you mean?"

Alik shrugged, looked out over the water. "Sometimes my dreams have really been visions of things to come. Many Arakkans have vision dreams." He paused and glanced at her. "Do you ever have them?"

Maran still stared at him, stunned by the sudden turn of questioning. "Well, yes, sometimes; not very often, though. And they're usually very trivial, like I'll do well on a test in my courses or I'll hear someone say a particular phrase. Nothing all that important. I haven't told anyone because it seems a bit silly, really." Maran shrugged and looked away from him.

Alik's voice was soft. "Maran, dreams are never silly."

They were silent as the sun continued its climb, then walked back to the cave for breakfast. Alik ate hungrily and Maran watched him with amusement.

She had barely even known him ten hours and already it seemed as though they had always been together. He had an odd sort of familiarity about him, and she had a sense that the two of them were more alike than she suspected. Maran smiled and shook her head. Being with him felt natural. With her other friends, even Iri, even her own mother, Maran had always felt as if she didn't really belong. For one thing, they all looked different with their bronzed skin and dark eyes. Rheet was the only person she knew with blue eyes, and that was caused by a genetic oddity on her mother's side. But no one had been able to explain Maran's fair skin, her regal features, and especially her violet eyes. She looked like Alik, and that was probably part of the familiarity. But with her other friends, she often felt as though they were inside somewhere warm and comfortable, and she was only looking through the window. She felt as though she were merely pretending to belong, that she was a stranger among these people she called friends. She had never felt she'd had a place in the world, so she had pushed herself to be popular, to be a good student, to be an exemplary friend. Now, for the first time, Maran was beginning to feel as though she really might have a place and really might have a friend— Aliksandar Pellen.

"What would you like to do today?" His voice snapped her back to reality.

"I thought we'd explore the beach some. The storm will have washed in shells from the atoll. We could find some real beauties. How does that sound?"

Alik nodded. "I'm game. When do we start?"

Maran shrugged. "Whenever you're ready."

He grinned and stood, trotting to the cave opening. "Last one out gets dunked in the water!"

Several hours later, the pair ambled down the beach, foot-prints and a serpentine drag mark from Maran's walking stick meandering behind them. Maran gazed down at her sandy feet. Alik gazed down at her. She had taken off her white shirt and tied it into a bag for their shells. Now, the sun beat down on her skin, dancing on her loose black hair, shimmering on her bathing suit, and Alik found himself thinking that possibly she was the most beautiful creature he had ever seen. She spotted another shell and bent down to pick it up, and Alik noticed his eyes memorizing the way her bathing suit stretched tight across her skin. Slowly, he knelt down beside her and laid his hand on top of hers. She looked into his eyes and he smiled.

"I see you've found a prize shell," he said, not even looking at the red and blue cone.

Maran cast a quick look down at it. "Ah, yes, I suppose I have." Her eyes wandered from the shell to his hand resting on hers. He rose with her, watching her move as she stood. Maran placed the shell into her makeshift bag and they continued their walk.

The sun was high in the cloudless midafternoon sky as Maran and Alik sloshed through the shallow water, Maran probing the sand before them with her walking stick. They had spoken very little; rather, they simply enjoyed each other's presence. The breeze felt gentle and friendly against their skin and Maran was utterly content. She silently admired the way the sunlight reflected off Aliksandar's well-built shoulders and back, the way his smattering of freckles seemed to darken in the light. And the way the sun played on his hair.

He's amazing, Maran mused to herself, not for the first time since they met. The thought had been a recurring one in her mind.

"Maran," Alik said softly, glancing at her, "tell me about yourself."

Maran chuckled and ran her fingers through her hair. "What would you like to know?"

He shrugged. "Tell me whatever you want. I'm not particular." He grinned. "You don't have to start with something as deep as religion if you don't want."

She laughed again. "Well, let's see . . . My name is Maran Ambora Thopel, daughter of Jinas Thopel, of Kalak Lar. I'm eighteen years old and I'm currently taking courses at Kalak University to become an officer in the Space Corps. I live with my mother and I don't have any siblings." She shrugged. "It's okay. It's not a big house, but I have my own room and I have a studio out back for my paintings. Mother thinks she keeps me on a tight leash, but she doesn't. I'm always sneaking out at night to walk on the beach or rendezvous with Iri. The city has a curfew and I'm really not supposed to be gone. Even though we've been on this planet for forty years, there's no telling what could come out of the forest at night. I've heard rumors of fierce animals living in there. And after my father's death . . ." She trailed off in midsentence. Alik could tell that it was a sensitive issue and decided not to ask. She continued, "The curfew has prevented our people from becoming just a bunch of midnight snacks."

Alik nodded and was silent a moment. Then he asked an abrupt question. "Maran, have you ever been in love?"

Maran blushed, grinning. "What kind of question is that?! Of course I have." She shook her head at the sudden change in conversation.

Alik continued to stare straight ahead down the beach. "What is his name?"

She sneaked him a sly grin. "His name *was* Ranul Gattran. We were together for two years. He was one of the best people I've ever met."

"What happened?"

Maran sighed. "His family had to move and he went with them. The last I heard from him was a year ago. I wrote to him several times. At first he wrote back, but then he stopped. I should've expected it, I guess. He had stopped signing his letters 'love' like he previously did. I really missed him. I didn't want to let go and admit that maybe we really were finished.

"He treated me like I hung the moons and raised the sun each morning. I never had anyone treat me that way and I really didn't want to let go, you know?" She looked at him questioningly, her hair blowing over her face. Alik nodded. "But now," she continued, "I don't hear from him anymore and I've given up on him."

"Have you found anyone to replace him?"

Maran snorted. "No. But, then, I haven't really been looking that hard either. Part of me doesn't want to admit that I

was wrong in putting so much into my relationship with Ranul.
It's so strange."

"Love is strange."

Maran laughed. "You're right there, Alik. You're definitely
right there. Love is strange. What about you? Did you leave behind a girlfriend?"

He smiled. "No. I have horrible luck with females. I don't
know if I expect too much of them, or if it's the other way
around."

Maran laughed. "What do you mean?"

Alik sighed. "Well, you see, when I meet a woman, I expect
her to be . . . well . . . understanding. I mean, I have feelings,
too, and a relationship isn't about being selfish. I respect her
and I expect to be respected."

Maran snickered. "That's a tongue twister."

"But you do understand what I'm saying." Maran nodded.
"Good. The last girl I was with wanted to wear me like a neck-
lace. She treated me . . . like a possession, showed me off to all
her girlfriends." He said the word snidely, and Maran had the
distinct feeling that he really wanted to say 'gossip group.' She
smiled faintly. "She bragged to her friends about all the things
we did and I just didn't like that. Nothing I said or did with
her was private. I couldn't take it, so I ended the relationship."
He shrugged. "Don't get me wrong, I'm not perfect. I've been
left."

Maran faked incredulity. "You? Left? Certainly not!"

He laughed. "Oh yes. I have not always been as . . . mature
as I am now." He laughed again. Maran smiled; she loved his
laugh. "The fact is, Maran, I am a walking catastrophe. Arrogant, selfish, spoiled, egocentric. You name it—that's me." He
pantomimed a weary sigh. "You might not want to stand near
me. I'd hate to be accused of corrupting you."

She grinned. "That's all right. I can deal with a little cor-
ruption. I'm a tough girl." She paused. "So what did you do
in Arakkan society? What was your niche?"

He sniggered. "My niche. Niches, actually. I began as one
of those chronically out-of-work painters."

"Really?" Maran shielded her eyes against the sun and looked up at him.

He shook his head. "Ah, yes, sad but true. I did good work; there just wasn't a whole lot of demand. The art galleries were full, or at least they claimed to be."

"So, what did you do?"

"Well, for a while I sold to offices and restaurants—such places always need new paintings. But there are only so many offices and restaurants, and they only have so much wall space, so I ran out of options in about a year. Then, Tahar be blessed, I actually got a real job, and, better yet, I had a lot of fun."

"Doing what?"

"Teaching! I took classes and I became an art teacher to a bunch of little kids. I adored those children." Maran laughed. "I wore real clothes—the school uniform—to look proper. I dressed the part. The kids loved me—Crazy Mr. Pellen that could sling paint with the best of them. We would sing in class; we would make up these really *bizarre* songs. You'd be surprised what a small child can concoct. Teaching was what I was doing when we were invaded. By that time, I had earned some respect in the community, and I ran for a chair on the local council. I won, and before much time had passed, I was dealing with the authorities. I even met the First of the Great Council. I became an adamant pacifist. While others wanted to take up arms and rush into battle, I lobbied for negotiation. Mainly it was for the children. I didn't want any of 'my' kids killed. I know they weren't really my children—I had no children—but I thought of them as a part of me because I had given parts of myself to them, and well . . . I wasn't about to let them be killed if I could do something about it. And when the pod mission came around . . . Apparently I had made enough of an impression on the First that I was chosen. It was a tough mission to accept, but I did it." He suddenly lapsed into silence. Maran decided to let it drop. She stared down at her feet.

"I've never really had a job," Maran finally said. "I paint, and my mother thinks very highly of me, and I've even won a contest, but sometimes I feel like I'm not doing anything with

my life. That's one of the reasons that I decided to go into the
Space Corps. I want to explore. I want adventure. Life is so monotonous where I live.

"It's so hard to grow up here. I mean, I'm an adult, but
people won't let go and think of me as an adult. I was raised in
such a tightly knit community, everyone treats me like I'm
their daughter. Even with Daken, Wix, Iri, and Rheet—we're
like brothers and sisters. I could never date Wix or Daken because I've known them all their lives. There's nothing left for
me to learn about them. I was there basically for every major
event they've been through. We've been together since we
were infants." She sighed. Suddenly, she noticed that they had
stopped walking and were standing together in the water.

Alik was looking at her very intently. His hand rested on her
bare shoulder. Maran could feel her heart begin to hammer in
her chest. *Calm down,* she told herself, but it didn't work.

"Maran," he said, his voice barely above a whisper, "Maran,
you are one of the most adult people I have ever met. In these
few hours I've known you, they have been some of the most . . .
complete . . . I have ever experienced. I feel like . . . like . . ."
He trailed off, shaking his head.

"Like we belong together," Maran said, finishing his
thought. Her voice was soft, like his. It was as though speaking too loudly would destroy whatever was between them.

He nodded slowly. "You feel this way, too?"

Maran began to walk again, slowly, Alik falling in step beside her. "Yes, I do. You are one of the most amazing people I
have ever met, Alik, and I'm not embarrassed to say it. When
I first saw you, my breath was taken away. It was incredible."
She paused and shook her head. "My empathy toward you was
instantaneous. It was like we'd always been together, like I already knew everything about you, even though I didn't." She
paused again. "I knew then that if I could spend eternity with
you . . . it would be too short a time." Maran fell silent. Taking stock of herself, she was surprised to find her last remark
hadn't caused her to blush out of control. She knew he would
understand. He understood her. She looked up at him and discovered that he was quietly studying her, his gaze intense.

Slowly, he nodded. When he spoke, it was in a soft whisper. "The Fates have brought us together, Maran. It must be true. Some things are meant to be."

They neared the cave and went inside as the sun began its downward journey. The two had spent the whole day together on the beach, walking, talking, learning about each other. It had been a pleasant day. Maran laid out their shells in a corner of the cave, then went outside to shake the sand from her shirt. When she returned, she discovered that Alik had spread out a picnic supper for them.

They ate in relative silence. No words needed to be spoken; it had all been said. After dinner, Alik recited a few of the songs he and his class had written—those that he could remember— and they sat in the dim light of the electric lamp. Maran brought out her music player and put in a cartridge.

Alik smiled. "Would you like to dance?"

Maran nodded shyly as Alik stood; he took her hand and helped her to her feet. Then, to Maran's secret delight, he took her into his arms and held her close, swaying gently to the music. Her arm slipped around him and she laid her head against his bare chest as he held her hand in his. Maran closed her eyes and smiled contentedly. They danced through three songs before the music abruptly ended.

Maran sighed in disappointment. "That's it. No more music." She moved to turn off the recorder, but Alik intercepted her. Maran felt herself caught up on the wave of his intensity and as their lips met, she was overpowered by it. His arms coiled around her, holding her body in a tight, almost serpentine embrace. Maran ran her fingers up the back of his neck and into his hair, her hands stroking through it, caressing his face. His kiss was so powerful, so engrossing, that when his lips pulled away Maran could only lean against him and tremble.

"You're shaking," he whispered. Maran could only nod. He smiled and kissed her forehead. "You must be tired. Get some rest." Alik led her stumbling over to her pallet, where she sank to her knees. He knelt with her, pulled the blanket up around her, kissed her on the cheek. Maran slowly sank down on her back, Alik continuing to look down at her. Finally, he rose, standing over Maran. He turned down the lantern and replaced it on the sand. Then, he, too, got into his makeshift bed, pulling the covers up to his midriff. He smiled over at her, the dim lamplight glittering in his violet eyes.

"Good night, Maran. Sweet dreams." Alik turned over on his side, away from her, and Maran watched as he adjusted the blanket around himself.

Maran sighed and closed her eyes. She could still feel him against her, holding her. She wanted to be held by him and never move, never pull away. She loved the way he held her, so gentle but so strong. She loved how he felt against her, how his body moved against hers when they danced. She loved his gentle smile, his tender kisses, the sound of his voice, the rise and fall of his laugh. She loved his seemingly endless supply of conversation. She loved . . . him. The thought hit Maran full in the face; it was sudden and she was completely unprepared for it. At first, she even fought to deny it. But the more she thought about it, the truer it became. She *had* grown very fond of Alik. It felt right to be with him. She felt complete, unlike she had ever felt before, even with Ranul.

"Have you ever been in love?" he had asked her. Maran realized now that it had been but an excuse to find out if she was currently attached. Maran smiled to herself. *That little sneak.* She hadn't believed in love at first sight before, but now she had changed her mind. *"Have you ever been in love?"* His question echoed in her head. She sighed again. *If I haven't, I certainly am now.*

7

"Maran? . . . Maran? . . . Hello?" The voice wafted into Maran's groggy mind. It was familiar. "There you are. How was last night?" the voice continued, unaware that Maran wasn't fully conscious. Iri. It was Iri.

Her eyelids hauled themselves open and Maran's eyes sleepily roved about the cave. Iri knelt on the sand next to Maran's head, looking down on her friend. Sunlight poured into the cave and a new lantern shone brightly. Behind Iri, Alik still slept, tangled in his blanket. Maran yawned and sat up in bed.

"So," Iri continued, "anything happen that might be of interest? Anything I can tell the newspapers? Do any studies of alien anatomy?" Iri had a way of being what Wix called "subtly tacky."

Maran rubbed her eyes and ran her fingers through her hair. "Nothing happened, Iri."

Iri smiled smugly. "Then why are you blushing?"

Maran was suddenly awake. Quickly she darted a glance at Alik; he was still asleep, sprawled on his back. Maran sighed. She stood up and led Iri out of the cave and into the sunlight.

"All right, all right," she said and began to tell Iri of her first night with Alik and her discomfort at being alone with him. "I strongly considered walking home in the rain. But then he told me how glad he was that I had stayed and what it was like for him to wake up and see me . . . I knew I couldn't leave him. And then . . . he kissed me."

Her friend's eyes widened, but Maran shook her head. "Iri, I didn't let anything happen. And it was just on the cheek. Besides, I wasn't even sure I *wanted* anything to happen. I went to bed and fell asleep. Yesterday we did some beachcombing, talked quite a bit, and later last night we danced. Then I went to bed. And that was that."

Iri Makkaar looked at her friend for a long moment. "I keep my promise to you, Maran Thopel. I won't tell a soul. You have my word."

Maran grinned. "You'd better not tell. Where are the others? I thought they were coming, too."

"Actually, I told them we'd meet at your house. We need to discuss Aliksandar's future and we really can't have him there. It wouldn't be right."

"So you volunteered my home. Great. Let me get dressed and we'll head back. It'll just take a minute." She ducked back into the cave. She rummaged in the back of the cave and pulled on a different shirt and another pair of shorts. She heard Alik stir behind her and knelt beside him.

"Alik? Alik?" His eyes opened and he looked up at her. "I'm going to be gone for a while today. Will you be alright here by yourself?" He didn't reply at first.

"I really don't want to be alone," he finally answered. "I know you have your own world, but I feel so haunted in this place. I can almost hear the voices of the dead. And yet you drown them out, you are louder than they are. I know you can't stay, but I wish you could."

"I know. But I'll come back. I'll be back tonight, I promise."

8

Daken leaned back on the couch. "Play the tape, Maran."
Maran had run the tape to the correct position on her
way back to her home, and now she pressed the play button.
The group listened attentively to Alik's descriptions of the
Shlatlar's invasion and his belief in Tahar. They were especially
interested in his certainty that this was his homeworld.

"Well," Maran asked as Alik concluded his recorded speech,
"what do you think?"

Rheet gazed at Maran thoughtfully. "He said something
about remote monuments in the forest. If this really is Arakka,
it's possible that they would still be there."

"But why wouldn't there be monuments in the city? Where
did they go?"

"Oh, Wix." Iri sighed. "Don't you remember your galac-
tic history? When one people invades another, they destroy all
that culture's objects and buildings. Anything that pertains to
the other people is eradicated, including monuments, schools,
and places of worship. I'm not surprised all the temples are
gone."

Rheet continued her train of thought. "But don't you see? If there were *remote* monuments, they could still be in existence, especially if they were in a wilderness area. And if we can find one, that would prove he was right."

Wix shook his head. "Right about what? That the Frathi, *our forefathers*, invaded his world and slaughtered his people? That we murdered women and children and burned their homes? That we took over their cities and called them our own? Do *you* want this weighing on *your* conscience for the rest of *your* lives? I know *I* don't think *I* really would. There's nothing we can change about it. If he's right—and we don't know that he is—then we should let the past die. There's nothing we can do about it."

Silence descended onto the room. Daken coughed awkwardly. "But don't you think we have a right to know the truth? Don't you think Alik has a right to know if this really is his home?"

"Daken," Wix replied, "you know he wouldn't just quietly accept that the Frathi killed his friends. And that's what we would be saying, isn't it? That we're murderers? Good-hearted though you may be, sometimes the truth can cause more trouble than a lie. You've got to know when to keep quiet about something."

"Wix, I can't believe what you're saying," Maran said, her voice dangerously soft. "We have to know; we have a duty—a moral duty—to know the truth. Tomorrow we go into the forest and find one of those temples."

"I'm with you Maran," Daken said. Rheet and Iri nodded their reply. Only Wix remained conspicuously silent.

"Well, Wix, what'll it be?" Maran's eyes were hard.

Wix looked up at her from his hands and met her eyes. "I don't have to take part in this—but I will. It will look suspicious if I don't go. But that's the only reason why I'm going to get involved."

Maran slowly nodded. "Thank you, Wix. I appreciate it."

"Moving right along," Iris said lightly, "where is Alik going to live? He's twenty-five; he can't spend the rest of his life in a cave, now, can he?"

"We could have him move in with one of us," Rheet suggested. Iri darted a glance at Maran, who consciously avoided her friend's eyes.

"Won't that look a little suspicious, I mean, a guy suddenly appearing from out of nowhere?" Daken asked.

Iri shrugged. "No problem. We'll just say he's a traveler from Kalak Singh and he came to live here. That's believable enough, don't you think?"

The others nodded. "Where would he live? I certainly don't want him." Wix crossed his arms in resolution.

Maran rolled her eyes. "I'm the only one with a spare room in their home. He can stay here for a while. I'm sure Mother won't mind."

"Okay," Iri said. "Summary: Tomorrow we look for temples; Alik is a traveler from another city; Maran gets the honor of providing him with a bed." She smirked at Maran. "Are you going back out there tonight?"

Maran shrugged, trying to keep the color from rising in her cheeks. "I might. I don't know. Probably for a little while. He might be lonely."

Wix checked his watch. "If that's all, I need to go. Class starts soon and I need to get my books. I don't want to be late again; Professor Hatch is starting to take special notice of me."

Maran uttered a tiny gasp as she, too, checked her watch. She had completely lost track of time. "That's right! I had forgotten. Thank you, Wix, for reminding me. This meeting is adjourned."

The group left Maran's home and went their separate ways.

The campus bells rang; classes had begun. Maran heard Professor Taldan enter the classroom and set his books on his desk.

"Good morning, class. I hope you read your assignment." He paused to check the roll. "Let's begin with Miss Andlar. What did you think of Captain Malkas Dayton's decision *not* to conquer the Spalandi of Tarkus III in 3047? Did he do the right thing?"

Shiela Andlar took out her notes and briefly referred to

them. She brushed a lock of brown hair out of her eyes. "Obviously not. By *not* conquering the Spalandi, Dayton left himself open for the attack."

"Oh?" replied the professor.

"Exactly. This is a prime place to apply Baylar's First Principle: 'Act before you are acted upon.' By not acting, Dayton showed that he was not only weak, but also that he could not command a people."

"But what about Mandal's Rule: 'Speak with the tongues of ambassadors and bring peaceful results'?" another student asked.

Shiela Andlar continued. "That can be countered by Baylar's Second Principle: 'Words alone can be read as inability,' and Torgon's Rule: 'A man can become tied with his own tongue.' Dayton erred by not immediately infiltrating the Spalandi government with his own people and establishing control."

The professor nodded. "Very good impressions, Miss Andlar. Thank you. Are there any other thoughts on Dayton's decision? Miss Thopel?"

Maran hesitated. "I think Dayton did the right thing. He tried to set up relations with the Spalandi and become neighbors. He very politely requested that they share the planet. Unfortunately, the people did not want to cohabit and attacked. But I think it was only right that Dayton was not the first to pull the trigger. What if Terrat Du had been occupied by someone else when we came? What would we have done?"

Her teacher frowned. "Miss Thopel, that is not the issue in question—"

"But what if—"

"I believe we were speaking about Captain Malkas Dayton's discovery of the Spalandi on Tarkus III. Do you have anything more to add, Miss Thopel?"

Maran stared down at her hands. "No, sir."

The professor nodded. "Then let's move on to you, Mr. Larken. Tell us your opinion."

Maran tuned out the rest of the class. She needed to think. Alik was right, she was suddenly very certain. They were trespassing. The Frathi were murderers. Maran tasted bile in her mouth as she thought of the thousands of men, women, and children her people had killed. They had destroyed a race of people. A whole race. Gone. Thousands, maybe millions. Dead.

But how had they kept it quiet for so long? She flipped through her history book, back to the very first pages. There she found reference to a group of men and women who found Terrat Du. None of them had children. They had been implanted with devices that would prevent reproduction. And once they had established a settlement, the devices were neutralized. *So that's it . . . They didn't have children, so they didn't have witnesses to their crimes.* Once the Arakkans were conquered, the devices were removed, and children were born and brainwashed to believe that they had come upon this planet peacefully. The elders controlled and isolated the youth into believing that there were no other races on this planet because they had never seen anyone. Most of the children had been born within a few years of each other, and now the vast majority of the young population was in their late teens and early twenties. The military program had only begun recruiting about three years ago. No one would know about the Arakkans until the elders were ready to tell. And obviously they wouldn't tell the proper story. There would be no truth.

And what would they do to Alik if they figured out he was . . . Arakkan? The word sounded odd in her own mind. She could imagine them lynching Alik, the last of his race. Or burning him. Or—*no, I must stop this train of thought.* She wouldn't let anything happen to him. She couldn't. Maran loved him. She had to save him. But how?

Maran felt her palms grow sweaty. She was one person, and she would be unable to do anything on her own. Even her few friends couldn't make that much difference. Maran was seized by despair. How could she save Alik? How could he regain his world? And how did she know that he was correct about this even *being* his world? The bell rang and Maran fled to the sanctuary of her home. She needed to rest before returning to the cave later that night.

*　　*　　*

The house was quiet. Alone, Maran picked at her dinner. She wished Alik were there to keep her company, so she'd have someone to talk to her, but that was unreasonable now. He couldn't walk into the village by himself. She would have to wait until later. Maran couldn't risk being seen by anyone; she would wait until midnight.

She thrust her unfinished meal into the sink and went outside to her studio behind the house; Maran unlocked the door and entered. With a touch of her fingertips, the lights came up and Maran strode over to the night table where she kept some extra clothes. She had to go back. She had as good as sworn she would return. Alik would be expecting her.

9

Midnight. The twin moons rested on the horizon, side by side like giant eyes, watching as Maran topped the knoll and walked down to the beach. The breeze caressed her long black hair and Maran rubbed her arms, even though she wasn't cold.

What am I doing? Why am I coming back?

She knew why. She couldn't stay away from him. Ever since he had first looked into her eyes, she had been made a part of a bond. Spending the day without him had been almost excruciating. She could hardly keep her mind on her studies. Alik had wandered throughout her head and she had let him take her wherever he pleased.

She wondered how intimate he would want to be. If it were very intimate . . . that would be a completely new experience for her. Not even with Ranul had she done anything like that. He had never offered; he hadn't seemed even interested in the idea. But for some reason Alik was different. He had such presence . . . Even now, several yards from the cave's entrance, she could feel his presence—feel him waiting for her. She was like a helpless insect being drawn into a giant spider's web—the only difference being that she wanted to go. She wanted to be caught.

She neared the cave opening and her heart began to thud loudly in her chest. Maran felt certain that he could hear it, that she had already announced herself. Maran leaned her back against the cliff face beside the cave mouth. She could dimly see the glow from the lantern. At least she wouldn't be walking into darkness. That was somewhat reassuring. She tried to calm herself, to take deep breaths. Mustering up all her resolve, Maran entered the cave.

Alik sat cross-legged on the sandy floor, leaning over a book. He held it close beside the lantern and his lips moved as he tried to read the unfamiliar words. Maran assumed that when the Frathi had come, one of the first things the Arakkans did was to try to understand the new people, as a token of goodwill. That meant learning their language. Alik must be trying to refresh himself. She smiled at his diligence, forgetting the worries she'd had only moments before. But her smile quickly faded when she realized how trapped he must feel, how alone. Suddenly, she wanted to run to him, to embrace him and kiss away all his fears. She wanted him to know that no matter what happened, she was there for him, always. She would protect him.

Maran took a few steps closer. "Alik?" she whispered. He looked over at her and smiled. The light glowed against his bare chest and legs.

"Maran, I was beginning to wonder if you were coming back tonight."

She sank down on the sand, folding her slender legs beside her. "I told you I would return." She paused. "What are you doing?"

"I found some books, so I've been reading. It's not as easy as I remembered; Frathi was a difficult language to learn. We all tried to learn; it was sort of a symbolic neighborly offering." He gestured to the book. "Luckily I have pictures in this one."

Maran glanced down at his selection. The book was many

years old, water-stained from when the tide had been excep-
tionally high one summer. It was an old reader from Maran's
younger years. *Shara and Kinon in the Market.* Maran smiled
fondly, remembering reading aloud to her mother on warm
summer evenings. Her mother had wanted to throw it away
once Maran had grown older, but Maran could not bear to part
with the memories. So she had brought it here, to their secret
cave. And now, it was being read again.

Alik was watching her closely. She seemed tense, unlike her
usual self. He knew she must be thinking of earlier. He hadn't
meant to trouble her. But spending the day without her next
to him had been . . . horrible. He was relieved to see her again.

"Maran," he whispered. "Maran, why did you come back?
It's so late; you could've waited until tomorrow to visit. You
needn't have troubled yourself returning."

"Alik, I wanted to come back. I . . . I . . . ," she hesitated.
I need to be with you, more than I realized. But how could she
say that to him without making an utter fool of herself? She
looked into his eyes, trying to find a way, only to discover that
he already knew. He knew she needed him, and he needed
her—possibly even more. And in that moment, Maran saw
that everything would be all right. Alik would never hurt her,
never force Maran to do anything against her will.

Maran sat on the edge of his pallet, watching him. The
lamplight danced on Alik as he slowly eased nearer to Maran,
his gaze locked with hers. Aliksandar's mouth covered hers in
a quiet kiss. His arm slid around her, bringing her closer to him
as his lips continued to press against hers.

His mouth released hers briefly as his hand sought the first
button on the front of her shirt.

"Alik, wait."

He stopped, balancing himself on one elbow. "What's
wrong?"

"I . . . I don't know if I can do this." She sighed, looking
embarrassed. "I know I said earlier that I was ready, but . . ."

He smiled, nodding.

She laughed, relieved that he grasped her thought. "I don't
know if I can do this so soon. I mean, I've never done anything

like this before, with anyone. It's never even been offered to me. I don't want to be taking it just for the sake of taking it. I don't want us to be flesh against flesh; it's got to be soul against soul, or it just won't be right. Do you understand?"

His smile broadened. "I have much respect for you, Maran. I would never force you into any situation. Whatever you want, that's what I'll do."

"Just hold me," she said softly. "I just want you to hold me."

He sat next to her and she laid her head against his chest and closed her eyes. Alik pulled the blanket up around her shoulders and held her. He smiled as she nuzzled his chest with her cheek. She was so silent that for a while Alik thought that she had fallen asleep sitting up. He had almost dozed off himself when her whispered voice wafted up to him.

"Alik?"

"Yes?"

She paused. "I think I love you."

It was such a simple phrase, but Alik was sent to the heavens. He smiled, squeezing her.

"I know I love you, Maran," he whispered. He felt her smile against him. After a few minutes, he knew she had drifted to sleep. He rested his chin on top of her head.

"I love you, Maran," he whispered again before closing his eyes. "I love you."

10

"What shall we do today?" he asked.

Maran sat down next to him in the sand, her feet almost to the ocean water. "The others and I are going on an expedition into the forest. I was wondering if you would like to come."

"Of course I'd like to go. Is there anything in particular you're trying to find?"

Maran paused. She had been dreading telling him this. "Actually, yes. We are hoping to find one of those temples you spoke of when the others were here. We wanted to see what they were like."

Alik was silent. To Maran, it felt as if a rift had suddenly opened between them. She longed to take back her invitation, but she knew she couldn't lie and tell him she was simply going to spend the day in classes. Maran knew she could never lie to him.

Alik drew a long, slow breath. "So, you want to find the temples. You want proof. You don't believe me."

The words cut Maran like sharp coral on the beach. She

looked up at him so their eyes could meet. "Alik, that's not true. I do believe you. I don't know why, but I do believe you. But in order to convince others, we will need solid proof that we don't belong here. If there are any more Arakkans, then they should be helped. We could at least share our community with them. I can only hope that you can find it in your heart to forgive my people for what we have done. I can only hope that you can forgive me."

Alik watched her as, suddenly ashamed, she looked away. He drew her to him, holding her as the hot tears of shame and confusion slid down her cheeks. "Maran . . . sweet Maran. I don't blame you for what happened to my people. I never will. You were not even born when the Shlatlar came. How can you be held responsible?" He paused and stroked her long hair, whispering soothingly. "Maran, I'm sorry. So, so sorry if what I said hurt you. I will go with you today. I personally will show you where to find the temples. It's all right, don't cry. I haven't stopped loving you."

She smiled up at him, relieved that at least he didn't blame her. He really was a true friend.

"We need to leave before dawn in order to get into town under the cover of darkness," he said. "We can't let anyone see me; it would cause too much suspicion."

She nodded in understanding as he stood. "I think it's about an hour until dawn now. I'll get my things together." He disappeared into the cave. Maran, meanwhile, ran her fingers through her hair in an attempt to brush it. Just as she finished, Alik reemerged.

"Could I bring some of these books?" He held up a couple of readers, then tucked them under his arm.

Maran nodded. "If you'd like. I probably have more at home. That's where we're going first. I need to change clothes; I can't go into the forest looking like this. And I need to meet with the others." She paused and picked up the lantern. "If you're ready, we'll go."

"I'm ready," Alik replied.

11

Maran punched in her code and let herself into the Thopel home. Her mother was still in Kalak Singh; she didn't have to worry. She ducked into her room and quickly dressed in jeans, a thin, sleeveless shirt, and walking boots. She found a black knit shirt and gave it to Alik as he entered the bathroom to shower. It was one that Ranul had worn; she had hung onto it for sentiment.

Maran sat at the kitchen table and drank a breakfast shake while Alik showered and dressed. He emerged from the bathroom with his hair wet and slicked back. The shirt was a bit loose on him, but it looked good—better than it had on Ranul. Maran offered him a shake of his own and he drank it down quickly.

"You can sleep out in my studio," Maran explained, leading him through the house and out the back door. Once outside, they entered a small, one-room, one-bath guest house that served as Maran's painting studio. A daybed stood in one corner and Alik laid his clothes on a small table. All around them were paintings; most were completed but some sat unfinished, waiting for her to return. Maran stacked a pile of papers on her drawing table, then began to gather up her pencils and paints.

"I'll bring you food as often as I can, although I keep a bit stashed in the cooler there in the lavatory. You can eat that, at least until I figure out how to tell Mother. There're some books in the cabinet, drawing books and novels. You can sleep here on the daybed. The sheets are clean."

She picked up a hand-held transmitter. "This is called a hands-mit. It's used to contact people. I could call someone across the planet and talk to them using the hands-mit. It's easy to use: just press the buttons assigned to that specific location—the hands-mit number. Understand?" He nodded in reply. "Good. This 'mit is patched into the home system so you can call to the house if you need me to bring something out or if you have an emergency. Right now, I need to call Iri and find out where and when we're meeting."

Maran extended a telescoping antenna and pressed some buttons, holding one end of the half-circle-shaped unit to her ear and speaking into the other. From her end of the conversation, Alik gathered that they would meet near the western edge of town. And Maran neglected to mention that there would be a sixth member. She put down the antenna and laid the unit back on the table. She slipped past Alik into the bathroom and filled her canteen, grabbed her lightweight jacket, and opened the door.

"After you," she said, motioning Alik through. He stepped through the doorway and Maran followed him. She pulled the door closed and locked it behind her. Their journey into the forest was about to begin.

II

▲

THE
TEMPLE

12

"And just what is *he* doing here?!" Wix's angry question cut through the trees like a saw blade. "I thought we agreed it would be just us going on this trip, not him!"

Maran sighed and looked down at the dead leaves on the ground. Even at the forest's perimeter, the leaves were dense. Maran felt like a dead leaf; Wix's anger pulled away all her strength. She felt limp, lifeless. How long would she be able to fight him, to defend Alik? She would eventually run out of excuses, run out of arguments.

"I told him about the trip and he offered to be our guide." She met Wix's eyes. "Yandar, if anyone can find these temples, it's Alik. He was born here; he knows this planet. He knows."

Wix shook his head, the dappled sunlight playing on his brownish hair. "I can't believe you honestly think he's telling the truth. He's an alien, Maran. He wasn't born here any more than our parents were. He just wants to infiltrate Frathi society, maybe even to make a way for his people to take us over. There was no one alive when we came to Terrat Du. Why is it so hard for you to believe that? The Frathi would not kill anyone native to this planet. We're peaceful people. The Frathi are explorers, not butchers. We don't—"

"The Frathi did kill his people!" Maran screamed. "They're dead, Yandar! Dead, and it's all because of our parents!" Maran broke off, despair in her eyes. She felt Alik rest his hands on her shoulders and tried to draw strength from it. Her next words were so soft they could barely be heard, yet they shook the treetops.

"I never thought I would be so ashamed to be Frathi."

It was a simple declaration, but it seemed to tear into her friends. Iri and Rheet gasped and looked away from Maran. Daken could only stare dumbly at her. Only Wix looked on with grim satisfaction. Alik bowed his head in shame.

"If you want me to leave . . . ," Alik began. But Iri pursed her lips and shook her head.

"No, Alik. Maran's right." She turned to Wix. "If he really is native, he will be able to find the temples. Wix, give him a chance. Then at least we'll know. And that's what we want, isn't it, to know?"

The group was silent while Wix stared thoughtfully at Alik and made his decision. Finally, he nodded. "He can come."

Maran let out a silent sigh. She shouldered one of the hiking bags Rheet had brought for them as Rheet pulled out her scanner compass and began to adjust it. Iri turned to Alik.

"Do you remember where they are?"

"Ah . . . I believe there is one in that direction—southwest from here." He hesitantly gestured into the forest. Iri nodded curtly.

"Then southwest it is." The others shouldered their bags and they entered the forest.

They had been walking for three hours with no results. The group plodded through endless uniform trees. Alik and Rheet led the procession, Rheet with her scanner; Maran brought up the rear. The sunlight was dim and splotched on the humus of the forest floor; birds and animals called to each other in the constant twilight.

Maran found herself thinking how surreal this all seemed. It was if they weren't really even on Terrat Du—Arakka—at all, but some far-off forested world where there was never visible sunlight and the trees stretched on forever. She felt cramped in the immensity of the foliage—small, as though she were a bug wandering through someone's lawn. Always the crunching of their feet on the leaves, always the chatter of the birds and the tree-dwellers, always the dim drone of insects. The monotony made her head spin and the hair on the back of her neck stand on end.

Maran felt very rebellious, being here in the forest. Ever since her father had been killed by an animal in these very trees, the forest had been forbidden to all Frathi. Only loggers were allowed into the forest, and they were taken by heavily armed escorts. The youth were never allowed to just go exploring. They were breaking the law by being here, but in light of the reasons, it seemed a very small law to break.

She looked up at Alik leading the queue. He seemed almost regal the way he carried himself with such assurance, even though his clothes were far from those of a nobleman. Maran closed her eyes and imagined him clad in fine silk and leather and a long, flowing cloak, red with black trim. She imagined him on a throne atop a temple, staring out over masses of citizens, all praising him. Maran smiled to herself. No, he was merely a teacher, not a member of royalty. He wouldn't be comfortable ruling. Not Alik, who considered professional-looking clothes too confining. She chuckled under her breath. No, definitely not Alik.

But if he were to rule, who would rule with him? Who would be his queen? Suddenly, in her mind's eye, Maran was there on a throne beside him, dressed in red silk, a golden cord wound though her black hair. In her imagination, Alik took her hand and looked over fondly at her, smiling. She smiled in return, happiness threatening to burst her heart.

"My directional indicators are going haywire!" Rheet's sharp exclamation snapped Maran's attention back to the present. They had come to a halt and were standing among the silent trees, staring around themselves. Rheet was frantically adjusting her scanner, trying to find a new setting. "What are we going to do?"

Alik squinted into the trees. "We keep walking."

Rheet's head jerked up sharply. "But we won't be able to stay on course. And we won't be able to find our way home."

Alik smiled in what he hoped was a reassuring manner. "It shouldn't be much farther now."

Wix snorted. "That's what you said an hour ago. Two hours ago. Come on, face it—we're lost. This was a crazy idea and we're lost. Lost!"

Maran's happiness of moments earlier vanished and she turned on Wix in a rage. "Shut up, Wix, just shut up! I'm tired of hearing your complaining. You have done nothing but run Alik down ever since we found him and I am sick and tired of it! If you're so worried about being lost, *go home!*" She made a dismissing wave to the trees from the direction they had come. "Go! *Go!* Don't let us hold you back. And for certain don't let Aliksandar the alien hold you back. I would hate to think that I or any of us are *inconveniencing* you."

Wix stood, silently contemplating Maran as she seethed with rage and the others exchanged silent glances. "Maran," he said softly, "don't get so bent out of shape. I never meant to personally offend anyone, I just think we should be cautious, that's all. And besides—"

"I see it! Come on, I found it!" Alik's voice came from about fifty yards ahead of them. The argument forgotten, Maran spun around and dashed into the trees with the others, breaking off branches and scraping their arms. The birds and top-dwellers grew silent at the ruckus the five made. When at last they reached him, he stood pointing ahead to a clearing mostly obscured by trees. Immediately, Rheet focused on her scanner. Her eyes widened at what she saw.

"Gods of the Cloud, it's back on-line. The scanner's working again. And I'm picking up a massive energy reading. A pulsing of some sort."

Daken peered over her shoulder. "Where's it coming from, Blondie?"

Rheet didn't even bother correcting him. Instead, she looked up from her instrument and into the clearing. "It's coming from there," she said softly.

The temple stood fifty yards before them, in all its ancient glory against the dark backdrop of the trees. As they approached, they could see that it was actually a low, square steppe trapezoid with a sort of altar on its top. It was no more than fifteen feet high, but was at least five times as long and its depth disappeared into the forest. Foliage and young trees grew upon it, where the forest has propagated itself onto the temple. Mist clung to the temple's massiveness, giving it an ethereal appearance. A sort of slope was scooped out of the ground near the front of the structure. Cut into one gray-brown stone side of the temple was a large, ornately carved double door, and it stood at the foot of the slope. The door was probably also used as a loading bay.

Maran cleared her throat, breaking the silence that had descended around them like a thick blanket. "Are we going inside?"

All eyes turned to her, then shifted to and settled on Alik. It was as if now that he had proved himself correct, he was suddenly in command of their expedition.

"Yes. We go inside the temple."

Cautiously, silently, the six approached it. Alik led, as if by some unspoken unanimous consent. As they drew nearer, the energy in the air became more and more evident and they could feel it pulsing through their bodies. Rheet kept her eyes fastened to her scanner, her subconscious mind threading her feet around the rocks and patches of low grass that spotted the soil on the forest path.

Maran couldn't take her eyes off the huge monument. It seemed to pull her like a magnet, causing her feet to move of their own will. She could feel its energy, its power wrapping around her insides like a giant fist. She felt dizzy, overwhelmed; a tremendous heat flashed through her body. The forest seemed to bend and whirl around her. She stumbled and dropped to her knees. From a distance, she heard Iri's voice call her name, but Maran was lost in a trance. She raised her arms up, as if she were reaching for the ancient structure, her hands open wide. Then she swayed and toppled over onto the ground.

Iri immediately rushed to her side. "Maran! Maran, are you all right? Maran, can you hear me?" When she didn't get a response, Iri shouted to Rheet. "Rheet, something's happened to Maran!"

Rheet knelt beside her friend and laid her hand on Maran's chest. "Her heartbeat is very irregular." She paused. "Oh Sayluz, Maran, don't go into V-fib. Come on, don't do this."

Daken squatted beside her. "What's fib?"

Rheet nervously brushed a lock of hair from her face. "Ventricular fibrillation. It's where the heart rhythm gets out of control it's so irregular. Usually the patient—" Rheet broke off, her eyes wide. "Gods, no! Maran!" Frantically, Rheet tore open Maran's shirt and began pressing on her sternum. "She's arrested. Her heart stopped. Somebody give her breaths while I do this. We've got to get her back." Iri bent over Maran's head, tilted it back, and blew into her mouth as Rheet continued chest compressions.

Tears swelled in Rheet's eyes. "Maran, come on! Come on, don't do this! Maran! Maran! *Maran* . . ."

She lifted her quill and leaned back from the book, glancing over the words she had just written. They were a list of names, those lost in The Coming, the broken bodies of the slaughter, the eradication. At the thought of the thousands dead, she shook her head and looked up at the candlelit altar before which she knelt. She closed her eyes in prayer for the valiant souls who fought to protect their friends and families. She prayed she would not need to add more names to the list of the dead. Sadly, she once again immersed herself in her work, her list.

She did not hear the stealthy footsteps behind her.

She had no time to scream as the bullet tore through her flesh and shattered the back of her skull.

The pen left a jagged mark over the names as her lifeless body slumped across the page.

"...Maran! Maran, come on, come back! Maran, can you hear me? Please, Maran, please. Please." Rheet plaintively called her friend's name as she and Iri continued to administer resuscitation. Alik had taken Maran's hand and held it tightly within his own, as if he thought he could use it as a lifeline to keep her spirit grounded. But his face was almost as ashen as hers.

Aliksandar couldn't believe what he was seeing. Maran, lying dead on the ground when only hours before she had been so full of life. So full of passion. So full of love. What hand had ripped her soul from her body? What had caused this? Tears of frustration spilled down his cheeks and fell to the sienna earth.

"Maran . . . ," he whispered, kissing her hand. "Oh, Maran, I can't live without you. I can't survive alone here. Please, don't die . . ."

Wix touched Rheet's shoulder. "Rheetie, you've been at this for twenty minutes almost. She's gone. Let her go. She's with Sayluz now. She's happy." He knelt and put his arms around her. "Rheetah, let her go. Let her go."

Rheet was shaking as she slowly drew her hands from Maran's chest. Wix reached across her and closed Maran's eyes and pulled her shirt together. Rheet burst into tears, sobbing hysterically, taking Maran by the shoulders and shaking her.

"No! I won't let you! *No! No!*" she shrieked, her voice carrying through the trees. Wix, Daken, and Iri held her, their arms wrapped around her as if to shelter Rheet and each other from cold reality. They were in such shock, no one could speak. Silence hung around their huddled forms.

Alik sat on his haunches, staring blankly at Maran's lifeless visage. *So beautiful,* he thought. *Why didn't I tell her how beautiful I thought she was? Why could I never find the right words for her? All I could do was kiss her; that wasn't enough. She didn't know. She didn't know.* Abruptly, he looked up at the darkening sky. His face was twisted with anger and loss as he raised his fist to the clouds.

"Tahar! Tahar, how dare you take her! She wasn't yours. It isn't her time! Give her back! Maran, come back! Maran . . . *Maran . . .*"

Her name. Someone . . . was calling her name. But who? What had happened? The book. The names. The altar. A bullet—*Oh, I've been shot!* Experimentally, her fingers touched the back of her head. Nothing. *What? But I know I was shot. I know . . .*
     There it was again. Her name. Who was calling? The voice sounded so familiar. But it was so distant. *Must get to that voice. Must go back. Go . . . back. Go . . . back . . . back . . .*

". . . back. Come back, please, come back. Maran," Alik whispered holding her limp hand to his cheek, "Oh, Maran."
     Her lashes fluttered and a breath gasped through her lips. Maran opened her eyes and looked up into Aliksandar's ashen face. Their eyes met and a wild yelp of joy surged from him.
     "She's alive! *She's alive!*" He pulled her into his arms and held her to him, almost afraid to let her go. Shakily, she looped her arms around his neck and clung to him like one who has been rescued at the last moment from drowning. Rheet grabbed Maran's pulse and carefully counted the beats. The others could only watch, stupefied. Maran buried her face in the crook of Alik's neck in an effort to shelter herself from the reality to which she had returned.
     "Her pulse . . . ," Rheet said shakily, "is perfectly regular. She's okay." Rheet nodded dazedly. "She's okay. She's alive."
     Iri stroked Maran's hair. "Maran, honey, what happened?" Maran shook her head, still nestled in Alik's arms. Iri sighed. "It's okay, don't worry. I'm so glad you're back, Maran. You can't imagine."
     Wix looked up at the sky. The sun was beginning to set behind the temple; night would approach very soon. "We need to get home before nightfall. The forest can be dangerous after dark." The others nodded in agreement. Wix continued, "We

obviously can't have Maran walking, so we'll have to take turns carrying her. Alik, you can go first, then I will, then Daken. Iri and Rheet can carry our packs. Are we ready?" They nodded again. "Then let's go. We've got about two hours."

13

Iri punched in the code to unlock Maran's studio. She could never remember the one for the main house. The door swung open and she flipped on the lights as Alik carried Maran's groggy body into the cluttered room and lay her on the daybed.

"If you'll step outside, Alik, I'll change her clothes." Iri said, ushering him out of the studio. Per Iri's request, Alik exited the little building and Iri pushed the door almost shut. Minutes later, she opened it again and stepped outside with him.

"There's some food in the cooler in the bathroom; fruit juice and vegetables and stuff. She should try to eat, if she's strong enough." Iri paused, looked down at her hands, then back up at him. "Alik, what happened at the temple? Did you do something to bring her back?"

Alik shrugged. "I honestly don't know. But I do know that everything I said is true—I could never exist here without Maran's support. Iri . . . I love her. I honestly love her. And she loves me, she's told me as much. You can't tell anyone, especially Wix. He doesn't like me, and I wouldn't want his hate to carry over to Maran, just because she chose to associate with me."

Iri looked into his pleading eyes, nodded slowly. "I promise. You have my word." He smiled again and clasped her hand. "Thank you. Thank you so much." He turned to go inside to Maran, then turned around to look once more at Iri. "I'll see you tomorrow."

Iri mustered a smile. "Tomorrow."

Alik sat on the edge of Maran's bed, staring down at her. She looked so peaceful, her chest rising and falling evenly in the dim lamplight. He ran the back of his hand over her smooth cheek, then kissed her forehead.

"My beautiful, beautiful Maran."

Her lashes fluttered briefly, then resumed their quiet stillness. He sat for a moment more, then stood and exited to the lavatory. There, he quickly showered, cleaned his teeth, and shaved. Alik reemerged into the main room wearing his favorite black shorts, his skin still moist and his black hair damp. He crossed to the bed where Maran lay sleeping, then groped under the bed for another blanket. She stirred momentarily as he climbed over her and onto the bed, wrapping himself in the blanket so he wouldn't be sleeping under the same quilt as she. He wouldn't take advantage of her. He felt her relax and go limp as she slipped back into a deep sleep, smiling softly in her dreams.

She had turned in her sleep to lay against him, her cold cheek against his shoulder. He realized she was incredibly cold, even though the little room was rather warm. He turned on his side and felt her hands. They were cold as well. Gently, he rubbed her hands between his, trying to stir the warmth into them. He carefully rubbed her face. Soon, she was less pale. But he knew she had more time to spend recovering, and that time would be best spent by sleeping and being kept warm. That would possibly be the best and only medicine he could offer.

Alik lay in the dark, watching her. After the events of this afternoon, he almost didn't want to ever close his eyes. He had been so close to never seeing her again. Never hearing her whisper his name as he kissed her. Never seeing her smile, never hearing her dancing laugh. Alik buried his face in her dark silken hair and tried to shut out the rest of the world. *Only her.*

There was only her. Tears began to flow down his cheeks and disappear in her midnight mane. So close . . . He had been so close to losing her. Too close.

"Oh, Maran," he whispered against her. "I would give you anything that you would stay with me. My heart has so much to say, but my lips simply cannot find the words." He paused as the tears continued to stream from his eyes. "I love you. I love you, Maran, I love you, I love you, I love you. I can't say it enough. I wish you could understand. I wish you could know, could feel what I feel."

Maran stirred against his chest and raised her head to look up at him. She furrowed her brow as she noticed his tears. "Alik, you're crying." Her voice was still sleep-groggy, but it harbored only concern. She squinted in the darkness and pushed herself up on her elbows to look at him. "What's wrong?"

Alik smiled through his tears. "I was so afraid today when I thought you . . . died. The thought of never holding you again . . . My whole world was crashing down around me . . ." His voice trailed off to silence.

Maran looked at him for a long moment. "I died?" Her voice was very soft. Her eyes broke away from him and roamed searchingly about the room. He drew her to him and held her tightly. "I died?" She repeated, her voice muffled against him. "I don't remember it. I don't remember anything."

"It's all right. You're alive now; we're together. Nothing else matters. I just want to hold you forever." His voice was a low whisper in her ear, his lips softly brushing her lobe. She ducked her head to nestle against him once more.

"Alik, I feel . . . different. There's something inside of me and I don't know what it is, but it's trying to escape. I don't think I can keep it in much longer. I've never felt this way before." A pause. "It's like an ache, a pulsing. There's nothing I can do to control it."

He rose up on his elbow as she lay on her back, looking up at him. "How long have you had this . . . feeling?" he asked, his fingers stroking her hair.

She paused, thinking. "I didn't have it yesterday, that I can recall. And I didn't have it this morning. It must have been this afternoon, but I can't remember . . ." She sighed in frustration.

"What does it feel like?"

"It's . . . like a burning . . . It's not a sharp feeling, but yet, it's not dull either. A question. That's what it is, it's a question." She smiled, triumphant.

He furrowed his brow. "I don't understand."

"Do you remember when you were little, and there was some question that you had, like 'What makes the wind blow?' and no matter who you asked, it couldn't be answered to your satisfaction? Even if all the answers were correct, they didn't seem to be what you wanted?"

He nodded. "This is that kind of yearning feeling?"

"Yes," she replied. "It's right here." She placed her hand a few inches below her throat. "I don't even know what the question is, much less the answer. I wish . . ." She blinked her eyes sleepily. "I wish I knew."

Alik gave her a gentle hug. "You need to rest, Maran. You've had a rough day." He smiled at his understatement. "Get some sleep." He moved to kiss her good night, only to discover her eyes closed, Maran having already succumbed to a dream.

She lifted her quill and leaned back from the book, glancing over the words she had just written. They were a list of names, those lost in The Coming, the broken bodies of the slaughter. At the thought of the thousands dead, she shook her head and looked up at the candlelit altar she knelt before. She closed her eyes in prayer for the valiant souls who fought for their friends, families, their homeland. She prayed she would not need to add more names to the list of the dead. Sadly, she once again immersed herself in her work, her endless list.

She did not hear the stealthy footsteps behind her.

She had no time to scream as the bullet tore through her flesh and shattered the back of her skull.

The pen left a jagged mark over the names as her lifeless body slumped across the page.

14

Maran awoke with a start and sat upright in bed. Her heart was pounding in her chest and she was hyperventilating. Her eyes were wide as she stared nervously around the room, unconsciously searching for her assailant. A hand gently touched her shoulder and she screamed, turning to face her captor.

Alik pulled back abruptly, snapping awake and jumping at Maran's quick motion.

"Maran, are you all right?" he asked softly. His brow furrowed with concern.

She stared at him for a long moment, as though she didn't even recognize him. Then his visage began to take shape in her mind; she blinked several times, and seemed to return to reality. Slowly, Maran nodded.

"I . . . I'm okay." Her reply was slow and unsure, her voice shaking, unsteady. She lay back and pulled the covers around herself, as though seeking shelter from the dream. Alik lay down with her and gently wrapped his arms around her, holding Maran's trembling body. Dawn's pink sunlight streamed in

through the curtains and bathed the room in a dim, warm
glow. It was a warmness Alik tried to transfer to Maran's shaking body. He closed his eyes and, smoothing her hair, tried to
soothe her.

Maran lay next to him, her face buried in his chest, her mind
trying to decipher her dream and make sense of the images. It
seemed that she had dreamed that dream before, but she
couldn't remember exactly when. It wasn't that long ago, not
more than a couple of days before. And it seemed for some reason that the dream had not come at night. But if it hadn't come
then, when had it come?

Suddenly, she remembered. Everything.

"The temple," she whispered, her eyes growing wide and a
gasp catching in her throat.

Alik frowned and opened his eyes. "Hmmm?"

Maran sat up again, the blanket falling from her body. "The
temple. Alik, we have to go back to the temple."

Alik sat up with her, his arm around her bare shoulders.
"Maran, no. You died there yesterday. I don't think it would
be wise to repeat that performance. In fact, I wish you would
see a doctor today."

Maran shook her head. "No doctors. I don't want to have
to explain why I was breaking the law by being in the forest. I
don't want to have to explain about you." She sighed. "You
don't understand. Something happened there yesterday. Something in my spirit. Alik, I became someone else. I had a book
and a quill and I was writing names in front of an altar—names
of people who had died. And I was shot. In the back of the
head." She touched the back of her skull. "Alik," she said, staring down at her hand, as if expecting to see blood, "Alik, I have
to go back. I must find out what happened to me."

Aliksandar regarded her silently. Quiet determination was
etched into her features, but along with it was something
else: fear—fear of what had happened, fear of what she could
find, fear of what might happen again. But she was right—
she had to know the truth. And, furthermore, he also had to
know.

He gently took her chin into his hands and gazed into her

beautiful violet eyes. "If you need me, I'll be there," he whispered.

Softly, Maran smiled and ran her fingers though his hair as he kissed her. Maran smiled against his lips as she pulled him back down with her to the sheets.

The hands-mit buzzed insistently. Alik groaned, reached behind himself to the night table, groped for a moment, then brought the 'mit up to his ear. He extended the antenna and rolled onto his back. Maran leaned against his side, smiling lazily and tracing little designs on his chest.

"Hello?" he said hesitantly, unsure of how the 'mit operated. He paused for a moment, then spoke again.

"She's right here. Just a moment."

Maran took the hands-mit from Alik and sat up, trying not to yawn. She finger-combed her hair as Iri began speaking.

"Maran, how are you feeling?" Iri's voice asked. "How did you sleep last night?"

Maran rubbed her eyes. "I'm okay. I'm fine."

Iri's disembodied voice sighed in relief. "Wonderful. What are your plans for today? Are you staying in, recovering?"

Maran paused, hesitantly, as Alik drew his fingers down her spine. She arched her back at his touch and grinned at him over her shoulder. "Actually, Alik and I were just talking about returning to the temple."

"Maran! Are you sure that's wise? He's the only one that could go with you; we've all got classes again today. Something might happen."

Maran rolled her eyes. "Iri, it'll be okay. Trust me, it will. And I'm going to skip class. I'd skip if I were recovering, so I'm going to just be absent. No one will care."

Iri sighed again. "Okay, okay. You know I just don't want anything to happen to you. Maran, you are my friend after all. I don't want to lose you." She paused before continuing. "By the way, where did Alik sleep last night?"

Maran grinned to herself. "He slept just fine," she replied. "I'll talk to you later. 'Bye." Maran disconnected the hands-mit without waiting for a reply.

"What did Iri have to say?" he murmured.

Maran slid onto her back. "She didn't want me to return to the temple."

It was a simple statement, and at first Alik wasn't even certain that he was supposed to respond. When he did, his words were carefully measured. He recalled her previous forcefulness; he wanted to be very careful not to offend her. "Maran," he said softly, "I wonder if she may be right." He paused, waiting for her reaction. When none was forthcoming, he decided to continue. "Remember, if you . . . die . . . again, I wouldn't know how to bring you back. If you die . . ."

"Alik, stop it." In one fluid movement, Maran was out of bed. She stood in all her sleep-disheveled beauty and stared exasperatedly at him. "We've been over this, so just cut it out," she continued. "I'm not going to die and that's that." She paused, then smiled impishly. "Besides, if I do, then I'll have to admit I was wrong." She moved to the night table, pulled out some clean clothes, and began dressing.

"We need to leave soon before too much of the day is lost." She pulled on her socks as he sat up and ran his hand over his hair. She looked up at him from her seated position on the floor. "Do you want me to step out while you dress?" He grinned and the tips of his ears turned red. Alik shook his head and chuckled.

"Or, I know," Maran continued, "why don't I find us something to eat?" She stood and wandered into the lavatory where the cooler was and rummaged about inside it. She reemerged into the room, food in her arms, and dressed in hiking pants and a loose, sleeveless shirt. He had finished dressing and she handed over pieces of fruit and a chunk of bread.

He smiled and quickly began eating. "You said we needed to leave soon. At what time?"

"Whenever you're ready," she replied.

"I'm ready now."

15

The temple loomed over them again; though less menacing than before, it was certainly no less impressive. The sun watched them from high in the noon sky as Alik approached the door. His hand rested against the large circular latch; he glanced over at Maran.

"Are you all right?" he asked.

Maran smiled a tiny smile. "I'm still among the living," she replied.

"Then here we go."

He pulled the door open and the two stepped back a few paces. Musty air whooshed from within and clouds of dust surrounded them. Maran coughed and waved her hand to try to dispel the dirty atmosphere. Alik turned on the lantern and held it up, shining it into the shadowy hall. Maran unconsciously took hold of Aliksandar's free hand; he squeezed it reassuringly.

"If you want to back out of this, that's fine with me. I'll understand if you decide you don't want to do this. Really, I will. Like I said, if you do that dying episode again . . ."

Maran shook her head, conviction etched in her face. "No,

I'm going in there." With determination, she stepped through the doorway, still holding Aliksandar's hand. He followed her into the massive monument.

The two walked hand in hand down a long, smooth-walled corridor. The walls, which were made of highly polished stone, leaned inward a bit, giving the hall a triangular sense about it. Dark creatures scurried past them in the dim light of the lamp and Maran tightened her grip on Aliksandar's hand. She was frightened, it was true; but having a friend here with her helped to diminish the anxiety that clutched at her throat and pulled at her stomach like a twisting fist.

They had reached the end of the hall and Alik held up the lantern to examine the wall where the hall split off into two branches. There was a large carving in the stone, one of a wizened old man with long wild hair and a flowing beard. His eyes blazed with knowledge and power and it seemed to Maran that he could leap off the wall.

"Tahar," Alik breathed, dropping to the ground. He released Maran's hand and bowed down before the carving, touching his forehead to the earthen floor. He rose back up on his knees and stared reverently at the artwork.

"Tahar," he repeated, motioning toward it. "He saved us." A pause. "Well, some of us. Those who were fortunate." He sighed and stood. "I'm sorry." He shook his head. Alik looked up at Maran only to discover one thing—she had vanished.

"Maran?" Bewildered, Alik turned in circles, staring around himself and wondering where she could've gotten off to so quickly. Panic rose in his voice. "Maran?" Aliksandar's eyes grew wide as his mind began going through all the things that could've befallen her. The hall branched into two passages running opposite directions; he had no inkling as to which one to take. "Maran!" he shouted again. "Maran! Maran!" He was growing desperate. He finally decided to try the right passage when a scream echoed from the left one.

Alik raced down the passage, lantern flopping at his side. He collided with her as she screamed again, dropping her little pocket flashlight. Alik wrapped his arms around her as she staggered and almost fell. Maran buried her face in his chest and began to sob, her body shaking uncontrollably.

"Maran, what happened? What's wrong?" Alik tried to pry her loose to look her in the face, but she clung to him like a second skin.

"Alik," she squeaked, "oh, Alik, it was horrible. She was so rotted and it was just like I thought, and I knew that she was who I had been and I thought, oh gods, no—but there it was and—"

Alik took her by the shoulders and peered into her face. "Maran, slow down. Tell me exactly what happened. Slowly."

Maran shook her head adamantly. "It was too horrible. Alik it was just like from the dream, just like from last night when I woke up this morning, just like—"

"Maran, you're rambling. Slow down." Alik tried to calm her again, hugging her close.

"Alik I'm sorry but I just can't stop seeing her face, her vacant eyes, her teeth, her body. Alik, oh gods, oh gods," she wailed, shaking her head and squeezing her eyes shut.

He took her face into his hands and held it still. She was making herself crazy and he had to break her destructive train of thinking. She had obviously been through a great trauma, but he didn't know what to do. He couldn't even kiss her and make it better. Could he? He decided to venture a try. Still holding her chin in his hands, he drew her to him in a deep, consuming kiss. Her arms slid around his neck and she tightened her grip on him as though he were a lifeline to reality, to sanity. When they finally broke away, Maran leaned against Alik, sniffling, trying to regain her composure and bring order to her thoughts. Finally, she found she could stand on her own and began to lead him back down the hall as she spoke.

"It . . . she . . . was from my dream, the one I dreamt this morning that scared me so. She's just like I remembered her. Alik, I'm frightened. Really frightened. I can't understand what's happening to me."

Alik protectively put his arm around her shoulders. The lamp shone its falsely cheerful light in an orb around them, but it brought no comfort. Thunder growled outside and the ground trembled as lightning struck somewhere close. Both knew without speaking that a raging storm was going to be upon them and they would be trapped in the temple until it blew past. It was not a happy prospect. The hall twisted a bit and dipped slightly downward. Strange carvings were spread across the walls, carvings that baffled Maran but that Alik understood as though they were childish script. There was a feeling in the air that Maran couldn't put her finger on, but it was similar to the one she had experienced yesterday, before she fainted. This time, though, she didn't feel dizzy, just . . . charged. It was the only word she could think of to appropriately describe the electrical sensation that coursed through her body. All her awarenesses seemed heightened: her hearing, her sense of smell, her sight. Maran's skin was hypersensitive and it was all she could do to stand Aliksandar's touch, but she couldn't cast his arm away—she needed his support, his strength. She needed him.

They rounded one more bend and came to another branch in the halls. Here, though, against the wall, was a sort of altar. It was made of polished wood and rose almost to the ceiling. Rows of cobweb-covered candle stubs stood on either side of Tahar's carved face and ran down to a shelf where a book lay open, words neatly written on its yellowed, brittle pages. And kneeling on the floor, fallen across the book, slumped the decayed body of a woman.

She was dressed in a black ceremonial gown with red and blue embroidery winding across the shoulders. The side of her face was visible as it rested where it had landed on the page, patches of leathery mottled skin still stretched over high cheekbones and around dark, vacant eye sockets. Yellowed teeth grinned from a mouth picked lipless by time. Her nose had vanished; a flap of aged skin stretched over a nub of cartilage was all that remained. Stubborn strands of black hair still clung to her head. The back of her skull had been shattered by a blow.

"That's her," Maran whispered after a long pause.

Alik looked over at Maran. "Are you certain?" His voice, too, was very soft, as though he was almost afraid he could wake the dead woman.

"I'm positive. This is her. This is who I became. Yesterday

when I . . . died. This morning in my dream. This is her. This is me." She was silent again as she continued to stare at the deceased figure, Maran's eyes as unblinking as the lifeless woman's. She studied the words written on the parchment, noticed the jagged ink mark that skewered through them.

"Those are the names," she whispered, "of people who died in the war. She was writing them down—chronicling them—when she was shot." A pause. "When I was shot." Another pause as Maran looked up at Alik.

"Who was she?" Maran asked him. "With her gown and this altar—she must've been someone. . . . Wouldn't you think?"

Alik let out a deep breath and rubbed his cleft chin. "She was most definitely someone, Maran. She was a high priestess, possibly even of the rank of Umak'Daahl. In any case, she was a top-ranking official in the Holy Order. For you to be flashing into her life, her last moments, has great relevance. I only wish I knew what it was."

Maran digested his words before speaking again. "We should explore more of this place. I can hear rain on the stone roof overhead, and I can hear thunder; we won't be able to go home yet. We may as well use our time wisely. Maybe we can discover something, find a clue."

Alik nodded. "It's worth a try."

Without speaking, Alik took Maran's slender hand securely into his own. The pair turned away from the priestess and ventured down the dark waiting hall into the silent unknown.

16

Later, even the lantern had given up being cheerful. Its light was now more one of resignation, of knowing that it had a job to do and it may as well accept that duty. The death it had seen had depressed it almost as much as the two figures whose path it lit.

Aliksandar's arm was around Maran's drooping shoulders, her arm around his waist. Some hours earlier they had left a room that had been entirely converted from a huge, grandiose worship hall into a torture chamber. Maran had become nauseous and wept on the floor at the sight of the crematorium ovens and tiled tombs of gassing rooms. In a smaller connected room were a row of shackles, now abandoned. As her mind reflected on what she had just experienced, Maran realized she had never seen such a horrendous and ghastly sight in all her life.

She knew why these rooms had been built. The Arakkans had dared to defy the Frathi and so the Frathi attempted genocide. The people were gassed, then their bodies burned, their ashes thrown into the forest. She knew this had been done before, in their ancient past.

In one section of the room was a series of bookshelves.
Dusty albums stood lined in rows, like columns of soldiers
standing guard over the remnants of their tyranny. Though she
really hadn't wanted to do so, Maran felt she had to read their
words, to at least glimpse into the horrible past. What she discovered made her even sicker. Where only Alik had been able
to read the words in the priestess' book—Maran being ignorant of the language—she could read the names in the album
with ease. Name after name after name: endless lists of men,
women, and children long since dead. Each name was accompanied by a photograph of the deceased taken just after the
spirit had departed the body, yet with the lifelike terrified ex-
pression still in place. It was appalling. She leafed through the
pages with a vacancy in her eyes, seeing but not seeing the
words and faces.

Alik peered at the book from behind Maran, his hands resting lightly on her shoulders. He couldn't physically help her
pass through this trauma of discovery, but he could be there
for her emotionally. He began to wish that he had never returned home, never stirred up the past, never brought Maran
such pain. And, yet, the pain was his as well. Though her people were the killers, his were the murdered. His friends and family were the ones who had been in these rooms. But he had
prepared himself for finding the elements of their destruction.
When he was chosen to be a part of the pod mission, Alik knew
that he may never see his people alive again.

Maran gasped and began to tremble violently. She rocked
her head back and forth, her hair dancing around her head. She
dropped the book on the table as if it were a hot iron and
backed away from it. Keeping his hand on Maran's shoulder,
Alik scooped up the book and studied the page. What he saw
made his mind reel.

Eyes wide and unblinking in death, his head held up by a
soldier's gloved hand, a man that could have easily been
Maran's twin brother stared out from the page. His eyes were
a bit closer together, his chin a bit more rounded, but other
than that the resemblance to Maran was striking. The man in
the picture was at least thirty.

Alik pulled Maran to him and turned away from the book, laying it back on the table. She was sobbing hysterically, shaking beyond control. Finally, Maran sank trembling to the floor, clutching at her stomach. Alik sat with her and leaned against the wall as she cried, her black hair a curtain around her face. Here and there he made out a sentence or two that she wailed, questioning herself and reality.

Aliksandar didn't know what to say. All the strain, all the stress from the past few days came pouring out of her. For almost twenty minutes waterfalls of tears streamed from her eyes. Finally, they began to lessen and her sobs came in jerking hiccups.

"Why?" Maran whispered between sobs. "Why is this happening to me? What does it mean? Alik, what does it mean?"

"It means my people were slaughtered," he whispered, tears finally making their way down his cheeks. "It means that I was right, and this really is my world, and . . ." He broke off. He was about to say, "And your people slaughtered my family and friends," but he knew that wouldn't be right. This wasn't Maran's fault. He was shaking now, the tears coming freely as he realized that he may never see his race again, that he might be the last.

"Maran, I don't know what to do," he moaned. "If I knew they were alive, then I might have some idea. But I don't know whether they are alive; it's possible that they are dead."

She sat up to look at him. Her face was somewhat swollen from crying, as were her red-rimmed eyes. Her dust-covered cheeks were streaked by her meandering tears. She sniffled and wiped at her eyes with the back of her hand.

"We have to keep going," she said at last. "I know we're both wrecked, but the answers are out there somewhere, and now we have to find them."

He nodded silently, brushing away his tears with his hand and arm. After a moment, she stood, and Alik stood with her.

"Let's keep walking," she said as they exited to the hall, hoping to leave the terror behind.

After leaving the chamber, they traveled down a dark passage, supporting each other, emotionally and physically. Both were silent as the lamp cast its grim light around them, throwing menacing shadows on the slanting walls.

They came to a series of small rooms, each with a cot, a worn chair, and a table on which a single candle stood. The two entered one of the rooms, and Maran immediately lay down on the cot and Alik pulled the chair next to the bed. He dug through the drawer in the table, found some matches, and lit the candle. Then he turned off the lamp to conserve the battery; he leaned back in the chair, letting out a long sigh. It would be best for them to rest for a few minutes, and then move on. They had covered about three floors of the temple, floors which were actually basements. At one point he mused that the water table must be very low here.

They sat in silence for a few moments, and Alik brought out a small sack of sandwiches they had packed that morning. They ate, and then rose, extinguishing the candle and turning on the lantern. There were still a few more floors of the temple they had to cover.

17

Outside the temple, the rain had begun to diminish. Sunlight fought through the clouds to spread itself over the forest and the temple. Birds in the treetops began to twitter almost experimentally, as though unsure if they were safe from the storms. Animals ventured from their homes to drink and play in the pools of standing water. The forest returned to life, oblivious of the ages of death within the temple.

The footstep was so soft, it was almost inaudible. The dark-robed figure stood in the hallway, studying the man and woman walking a few yards ahead of him. His eyes took them in, absorbing their shapes in the light of his candle as a sponge absorbs water. He took a step closer, the candle's flame mingling with the lantern's light, their glow throwing strange dancing shadows on the walls. The figure cocked his head, curiously, as he watched the two figures.

"Someone. Someone else, someone." The words were whispered in the strange clipped tone of one whose sanity fled long ago. "They've come back. Come back again. Again." The figure's eyes grew wide in his wrinkled face. A grin cracked through his lips. "Back again. Saved, we are saved, we are. Saved." His voice rose in excitement. "The Coming. The Coming! We are saved!"

Maran spun around with a start. She yelped at the sight of the wild-looking man behind them. Equally startled at her outburst, the man took a step backward, raising his free hand. Maran yelped again and Alik placed his body between Maran and the strange man. For a moment, no one moved. The air stilled and the only sound was that of breathing. Then, Alik spoke.

"Who are you?"

The man took a hesitant step forward, his hand still raised to protect himself. "I am of the Holy Order. I serve Tahar, always, Tahar." He gestured to his ragged robe and Maran could see that it was much like that which the priestess wore, with its blue and red embroidery. "You have come to save us, yes? You will banish the Shlatlar, yes?" He nodded eagerly, causing the wispy strands of wild gray hair to wave and dance around his head.

Alik hesitated. "My name is Alik and this is Maran." He paused. "How exactly would we save you?"

The man nodded again. "You will save us."

Alik shook his head. "Why do you say that we will save you?"

"Save us, save us, yes, yes. The Shlatlar are coming, breaking through. You, you will save us from them."

Alik sighed in frustration and glanced at Maran. She shook her head. He decided to choose another approach. Looking pointedly at the man, Alik tried another question.

"What is your name?"

The man paused, studying Alik suspiciously. "Name? My name? Why do you want to know?"

Alik was baffled by the question. "So we will know what to call you."

The man nodded, still considering them. "You do not want

to know for the catalogs, the books? You do not want to know for the lists?"

Alik furrowed his brow. "The lists?"

"He means the lists of the dead," Maran whispered, "like the one the priestess was making." She paused, then addressed the man. "We are not collecting names for the lists of the dead, we are counting the living. You are a survivor; we need to know your name."

The man smiled at her. "Daughter of Teerla. Beautiful girl. Tahar's child, beautiful child." His smile widened. "I am Parthul. Parthul. Parthul." He repeated his name over and over, laughing, as though he hadn't said it in so many years that he had almost forgotten how it sounded.

Alik smiled. "Parthul, are there any others like you, any other survivors?"

Maran laid her hand on Aliksandar's shoulder. "Alik," she whispered. "Maybe you shouldn't ask this just yet." She didn't want him to hope for something that might not be, especially since Parthul seemed less than grounded in reality.

Alik shook his head. "No, Maran, it's all right. Really." He recentered his attention on the man. "Parthul, are there any others like you, any other survivors?"

Parthul nodded gleefully, excited at the prospect of some-one using his name. "Others, yes, yes. In the village. There." He pointed toward the southern wall of the room. "The vil-lage is there."

Maran cocked an eyebrow and glanced at Alik. "Parthul," she asked, "can you take us there, to the village, to the others?"

Parthul began to speak but caught himself. "No, no, no. Cannot take you. Cannot leave the temple. Tahar. Must stay with Tahar. Cannot leave temple." He shrugged apologetically. Alik sighed in frustration. Parthul continued, "But I have a map, yes. Map to village, to others. Will show you, yes. Come, show you map." He turned away and shuffled from the room. Alik and Maran stood quickly and, grabbing their lantern, fol-lowed the candle's glow out into the darkness of the waiting hall.

*   *   *

They had been following Parthul's shuffling gait for an inde-
terminable length of time. He mumbled to himself in his odd,
rising-falling voice about the Shlatlar, about being saved, about
Teerla's daughter. Each time the girl was mentioned, he cast a
quick, sidelong look at Maran and smiled gleefully. Maran
began to get a crawling sensation along the back of her neck.
Her hand sought Aliksandar's and held it.

"The map is just here, in this next room," he smiled as he
waved his hand at the bend ahead of them. "I will show you,
yes, how to find the others. They will welcome you, yes, be
overjoyed." His last sentence was accompanied by a high laugh
and a wild grin. Maran and Alik smiled uncomfortably.

Parthul entered the room around the corner, but Maran
held Alik back.

"Alik, we have to discuss something. There is the possibil-
ity that he could be . . . well . . . wrong." She paused at his
frown. "What I'm trying to say is, you and I both agree that
Parthul isn't all . . . there." She raised her eyebrows significantly.
Alik nodded. "Well, there's a good chance that the village isn't
there anymore either. That he's been here so long that time has
passed him by without his knowing."

Alik nodded again. "I know. I thought of that. He's obviously living in his own reality. But he could be right. The only
way for us to know is to follow him and look at this map." Alik
stared meaningfully at Maran, then turned and entered the
map chamber. After a thoughtful moment, Maran followed
him through the arched doorway.

Torches lined the perimeter of the room. Parthul must have
lit them while Maran and Alik had their discussion outside. But
by the light of the dozen torches, they could see that the entire far wall was a huge relief map. Maran saw cities, rivers,
mountains, forests—all represented on the massive map. Upon
closer inspection she discovered that it was actually carved into
the stone face of the wall. Slowly, she approached it and ran her
fingers over the surface. Her mouth hung agape as she marveled
at its immensity.

"Yes, yes, the map," Parthul said in his singsong voice, gesturing expansively at the wall. "You can find anywhere on here, on this map. I will show you how to find the village, yes?" He nodded eagerly, looking to Alik and Maran in askance.

Alik nodded and Maran took a folded piece of cellum and pen from her belt pack. Parthul ran his finger along the raised bumps of the forest and along the plateau, jabbering semicoherently all the while. Maran followed his instructions carefully, writing them down as he spoke. Finally, he finished and turned to them.

"I have one thing to ask of you," his eyebrows rose with the query.

"Name it," Alik responded.

"You will tell them I am here, yes? You will tell them Parthul survived, yes? I have seen no one in so many, many years. Many, many years. I think they do not remember me. I think they do not know I lived."

"Why were you allowed to live, Parthul? Did the Shlatlar have a purpose in sparing you?" Alik didn't mean to be so blunt with his question, but he couldn't think of other phrasing.

The old priest looked saddened for a moment, but then regained his composure. "They wanted Parthul to be an example, to tell any who come of their power. They told Parthul I would starve, but I did not!" He seemed especially proud of this fact.

Maran smiled sympathetically at him, placing her hand on his arm. "Yes, Parthul, we'll tell them you survived. But why didn't you leave if you are the only one here? Why not go to the village yourself? Certainly they would have welcomed you."

Parthul drew himself up to his full height. "Surely these robes so fine show you I am a man of the priesthood. I could not leave. Never never! I would be deserting Tahar and I am bound to serve him for eternity. Eternity, eternity, eternity!" He smoothed his tattered robes proudly, obviously not realizing their state of ruin.

Maran's eyes widened. "You can never leave here?" She asked in amazement.

Parthul nodded proudly. "I will die here."

Maran was stunned by his reply. Alik explained. "When an Arakkan is inducted into the Holy Order, he or she takes certain vows. To bear a single child in the name of Tahar, to live by Tahar's word and teach that word to others, and to die on Tahar's sacred ground. Asking Parthul to leave would be asking him to break his vows to our god. We can't do that, Maran. Do you understand?" Alik asked her.

Maran nodded, having regained her composure after her initial surprise. "Parthul, I apologize if I insulted you in any way. I didn't know of your promises."

Parthul gave her a dismissive wave. "I am not insulted, no, Maran Child. You could not have been aware since you have been away so long." He smiled in his odd way. "Come, I will take you to the food stores, yes, so you may be on your journey. Come." He turned and shuffled toward the doorway, motioning to them all the while. "Come," he repeated in his singsong voice, "come, come."

Maran and Alik followed the priest down more winding corridors to another large chamber. Here, large bins and sacks lined the walls and in the back of the room was a pump for water. The two were given sacks to fill with dried fruits, berries, and nuts. Each was given a bedroll for nightfall. Canteens were refilled at the pump, hands and faces washed. Maran lightly wet her hair so she would stay cool during the hike to the Arakkan village. They finished their activities in what Parthul referred to as the pantry and were led back to the entrance.

"We would like to thank you for all you have done, Parthul. Maran and I greatly appreciate your kindness."

The priest smiled warmly at Alik. "I am but doing the will of Tahar, Aliksandar. May he be with you, yes, on your journey home." He clasped their hands and, bidding them good luck, returned to the darkness of the temple, shutting the door behind him. Silence was left in his wake. Finally, Alik broke it.

"What do we do now?" he asked.

Maran shouldered her packs, looking up at the sun, shielding her eyes. "There are only about five hours of daylight left;

I'd say we had better get moving. According to this map, we have about twenty miles to cover."

Alik nodded, shouldering his packs too. "I'll be right behind you."

III

▲

THE
VILLAGE

18

They had been walking for nearly four hours. The sun was sinking below the tops of the trees, throwing Aliksandar and Maran into a green-tinged twilight. Alik had found walking sticks and the forest seemed to echo with the monotonous sound of *crunch crunch thump, crunch crunch thump*—the sound of their feet on the humus combined with the plunge of their wooden poles. Colorful birds and wide-eyed treetop dwellers watched them curiously from their emerald perches. Maran felt the pressure of a thousand eyes watching her and it made her nerves tingle. She felt as if she could almost, not quite but almost, hear them whispering from their lofty seats. She sighed. Perhaps she was just tired and her mind was playing tricks on her.

Alik looked over at Maran. Her hair was pulled back in a ponytail, though her bangs were wet with perspiration and stuck to her forehead. Her sleeveless shirt stuck to her back. He could see the muscles in her arms working as she swung her walking stick. Still, the same determination that took her into the temple was visible on her face.

"Maran," Alik said, "tell me more about yourself. What is your earliest memory?"

She looked down at the ground but did not break her pace. "I remember when I was about two and a half years old—Iri, Wix, Rheet, and I were playing in a park near the forest boundary. Mother was watching over us, along with some of the other parents. I got away from her and took off toward the trees. When she caught me, I remember her saying that I should never go into the forest. She said bad things happen to people in the forest." Maran lifted her gaze from the ground and transferred it to Aliksandar's face. "My next memory is from several years later. Some of the children at my primary school teased me because I didn't have a father." She hesitated. When she spoke again her voice was very soft. "Mother told me my father was lost in the forest, but I've always wondered if she was telling the truth. Not really lying, just not telling the whole truth of what happened."

"What do you think happened to him?" Alik asked her.

Maran shrugged. "I don't know. Maybe he did disappear like she said. I just don't know." She sighed. "I've missed not having a dad. I've always thought that I would have been Daddy's Girl if he had lived. I can picture what he would've looked like—in fact, I know what he looked like because I've seen him in dreams. Dreams that—" She suddenly broke off, shaking her head.

"What?" Alik asked softly. He could tell she was upset, but he hoped talking about her pain could be therapeutic.

Maran sighed. "I've never told anyone what I'm about to tell you. I had a dream when I was . . . sixteen or so. My mother and my father were there, but my mother wasn't my mother. She had long black hair and she wore a long black dress. My father was dressed in black also. I was an infant and they held me in their arms. Mother was crying. A man in a strange uniform came to them and took me from my mother's arms. He put me in a basket and carried me away. Then I remember hearing—or feeling—screams." She paused. "And then I woke up in a cold sweat.

"That's the only dream I've ever clearly remembered. Anyway, I've always remembered that dream with my father as clearly as when I first awoke. It's never faded or gotten hazy; it's always stayed the same intensity. And I could see him, Alik . . . he was so real. Not only was I portrayed as an infant, but my . . . spirit, I guess . . . was standing outside of my body watching all of this happen. He looked"—her voice caught in her throat—"he looked just like me. His nose, his eyes, his lips . . . they were the same." She fell silent.

Alik let himself become lost in thought as they continued to walk in the fading light. He had to tell her something, but how . . .

"Maran—"

"Alik—"

They both spoke simultaneously, voices twining together. Alik smiled.

"Go ahead, Maran," he said.

Maran hesitated. "I've been thinking, Alik. Everything I've seen, heard, dreamed—it all points to one thing."

"And what is that?" Alik asked.

She hesitated again. "I'm not Frathi."

Alik stared at her. "Maran, are you sure?" He didn't mention that he had been about to point out the same observation.

She smiled. "No, it's just a hunch. But I feel . . . It must be true. I . . . I can't explain it. It's just a feeling I have. And it's a little scary." Maran sighed. "I'm tired; let's make camp here."

The two dropped their packs under a tree. Maran brought out the small bags of food and they dined by lantern light on nuts and dried fruit. The insects began their nightly song as Alik unrolled their beds. With a glance toward Maran, he opened them out and lay one just overlapping the other, making one large pallet instead of two smaller ones. As he worked, Maran built a shallow fire pit a few feet away, scooping away soil with a spade from a fire kit Parthul had given them, surrounding the pit with stones. Once it was built, she started a small blaze that cast a warm glow. Alik pulled off his boots. Maran did the same. They sat their boots together and tied a sack over the top, in order to keep insects out of their shoes. The two lay down and Maran folded one arm behind her head.

"Can you talk about this . . . discovery you've made?" He asked. "This assumption that you are not Frathi?"

Maran sighed and looked up at the treetops. She really couldn't see them, they were concealed by darkness, but her imagination created the outline of leaves and branches. Her voice was hushed as she spoke.

"That's all it is, really, just an assumption. An idle theory. And because of that, it's difficult to discuss. I'm still trying to deal with the whole idea that I may not be who I once thought I was. I'm trying not to have an identity crisis, and I'm trying to be rational, but I'm really scared. If my heritage has been a lie, how much else has been a lie? I've always wondered why I really never felt that I fit in with any of my friends. Even when we've been at our closest, I've always felt . . . distanced. It's like that with everyone—everyone but you."

"Maran, that could just be our attraction to each other. It doesn't mean that you—"

"But there's more," she continued. "The death experience at the temple, and then again this morning; you said yourself that the fact that I'm entering this priestess' last moments are significant. Maybe it's because I'm one of her people. One of your people, I mean."

Alik propped himself up and looked at her. What he was doing—playing the fool about something he had figured out long ago—he knew it wasn't right, but anything else would seem arrogant and presumptuous on his part. Besides, in order to make Maran completely think this through, he had to play the fool.

"So, you're saying that instead of being Frathi, you're Arakkan? Is that it?"

Maran nodded. "I know it sounds crazy. And trust me, I'm so scared of the thought that I've been living a lie . . . I'm surprised I'm so rational about this. But think about it. It makes sense. The way I look, my connection to you, my dreams—I must be if not full-blood Arakkan, then at least part. The fact that we have such a strong empathic link—we wouldn't have that if we were of different peoples, I believe." She paused. "And the man in that book of photographs, the one we saw in the temple . . .?"

Alik responded slowly. "Yes . . ."

"He was my father. I know it. I could . . . feel it."

Alik was silent. Maran let it drag on for a few wordless moments before she finally had to speak, to say something.

"What are you thinking?" She asked him.

He hesitated. "I'm thinking that you're right. He is." Alik paused. "Maran, you may be angry at me, but I've known all along that you were Arakkan. From the moment that I first saw you, I knew you weren't like your friends. I could feel it. I just wasn't certain as to what extent your differences ran. And I didn't say anything because I knew you had to discover this for yourself. I see now that your differences run very deep. Very deep indeed."

"Alik, if we do find more Arakkans, do you think they will have changed? Do you think they will be like you remember them?"

Alik lay back down, Maran curling up against him. "Everything changes, Maran. I know that the Frathi would not have let them stay at the level of prosperity they had reached when I left. Even as I was making ready for departure, saying goodbye to everyone, donating my finances to the war fund . . . I heard reports that entire cities were being burned to the ground and that the few survivors had built refugee camps in the forest. The conditions were supposedly very poor, but those were only rumors. My life was so hectic, what with preparations for the mission and leaving, going through physical examinations, that I am afraid I didn't pay as much attention as I should have to what was going on around me."

Maran smiled. "That's okay, Alik. You could hardly be expected to be on top of everything all the time."

"I know that. But, still, they are my people. Are. Listen to me. Are." He chuckled, though it was a humorless laugh. "I am building myself up, Maran, thinking that we'll find them, hoping that all will be as it was when I *know* it won't be. It *can't* be. Too much happened to them for them not to have changed. Part of me hopes . . ."

Her voice was soft. "What?"

He hesitated. "That we won't find anything. Because if we do, and they have drastically changed . . . I'm afraid that I'll be completely estranged from my own people. I'll have come all the way back, and not even belong in my own home." Alik paused for a long moment. "Home," he whispered. "I never believed I would say that word again."

Maran slid her arm over Aliksandar's chest and gave him a little hug. "Home is where you are loved, Alik. As long as we are together, you are home. Because I'll always love you." Her voice was soft, exhausted. Alik knew she needed sleep. He kissed the top of her head.

"Good night, my beautiful Maran," he said softly. "I love you."

"Good night, Alik," she whispered. "I love you too." Maran soon slipped into a deep, dreamless sleep. Some minutes later, Alik joined her in slumber. And in the trees, the night birds began their calls, emerging from their homes.

19

Maran heard voices, as if from very far away. At first, they were in a strange tongue, but then it seemed to change and she could understand the words. In her dream, she tried to understand what they were saying.

". . . While sleeping . . . not know . . ."

And another voice, this one deeper. ". . . Us . . .? Their hair . . . Sleeping . . ."

Then the first voice again. ". . . To the First . . . Answer . . ."

She heard the crunch of a foot on dried leaves and her eyes snapped open. Maran found herself staring up the barrel of a rifle and into the face of a young man dressed in an old vest and pants, with a red badge on his chest, his long black hair tied back. Maran could see that he was near her age, the time in his life when he was crossing over into adulthood. The other person, an adolescent, was dressed in the same fashion, and held a rifle on the still-sleeping Alik. Both of their faces were unreadable as they stared. Both had violet eyes.

Maran cautiously nudged Alik. "Wake up," she whispered, "and don't move."

Alik stirred and gasped as he saw the faces of their captors. *"Ail Tahar . . . ,"* he whispered in Arakkan, slowly raising his hands. *"Nyo toha ve Aliksandar Pellen, tyo toha ve Maran Thopel."* He gestured to Maran. The two men exchanged quick glances, still unsure of their prisoners' sincerity.

"What reason brings you to this part of the forest?" The man with the deep voice and the rifle directed at Maran asked this question.

Maran looked at Alik. "He speaks Frathi? How does he know Frathi?"

Alik waved her quiet. "We come looking for Arakkans. I am Aliksandar Pellen of the Pod Mission. I have been in space for twenty years. Now, I have returned home to my people. Please, would you take us to your village?"

"The Pod Mission . . ." Slowly the rifles were drawn away. Eyes wide, the man with the deep voice introduced himself as Prestun and his companion as his younger brother, Tamald. "We didn't realize you were of the Pod Mission. Yes, yes, you must come to the village. The First will most certainly want to speak with you."

"As will the Umak'Daahl," Tamald added. He and his brother stooped to help Alik and Maran to their feet, and then assisted them in breaking camp. In less than half an hour, the four were on their way.

The course varied from Parthul's map, as Maran expected, taking them southwest of the village he remembered. Instead, they poled up a river tributary, and walked to a large clearing in the trees. There, before Maran's eyes, were Aliksandar's people.

The village was small, with small houses which were made of some sort of prefabricated material. Each windowless dwelling was about eight feet tall and boxy in shape. Some homes had scenes painted on them; Maran saw chronicles of ceremonies and hunts from days past. There was a school building where children gathered near the town's outskirts and a worship center next to it; a meat house had been built over a

babbling stream shooting off from the river. In the center of
the village stood a larger dwelling, with many colorful scenes
painted on its exterior. As they approached it, Maran knew in-
stinctively that this must be where the First lived. Prestun
opened the door flap, leaving Maran, Alik, and Tamald to wait
outside the house.

Maran used Prestun's absence to further study the area as
the village began to come to life. Women and children dressed
in loose woven clothing emerged from the dwellings to begin
chores, like fetching water from the river and working spinning
wheels or looms to make fabric for clothes. Children stared and
pointed at Maran and Alik in their strange garments; Maran realized that she needed to get a hold of some of the local fash-
ions.

A hunter rode into the town center on the back of a verhi,
the black horselike animal's hindquarters painted with bursts
of red. Slung over the man's lap was a fresh kill, a black woolly
springer. Apparently, this one had not been lithe enough.
Thanks to the man's practiced shot, the beast's meat would feed
a family for weeks, the bones would be crafted into tools, and
the soft, thick fur made into clothing or bedding. Three women
crowded around him and carried off his burden, singing in
melodious voices about the hunter and his prey. A small flock
of five children ran along next to his mount, laughing and
reaching up to touch his hands. He and his little fan club left
the village limits to return his verhi to the herd in the field beyond. Maran could see more of the beasts in the distance, near
a smooth lake.

Tamald touched Maran's shoulder, gestured to the depart-
ing hunter. "He is Darryil, one of the hunters. He has killed
more springers than any of us—except the First, of course." He
paused, fingering the red badge on his vest. "He is training me
in the ways of the hunter, the warrior. Prestun is training, too;
he is doing much better than I. My brother says I should have
taken up with the painters."

"The painters?" Alik asked, coming to life, seizing the word
and wrapping himself around it. "There are painters here?
Where? Can I meet them?"

Tamald looked surprised. "Yes, there are painters. Who else would portray the stories? Who else would speak the images?" He shook his head. "The painters are as important to our society as the hunters, or the teachers, or the builders. They are as valuable as the gatherers or the seamstresses who make our clothes. They interpret the words of the Holy Ones, and record it for our future." He looked hard at Alik. "Are you a painter, Alik of the Pod Mission?"

Alik nodded vigorously. "Yes, yes, I am. I was a teacher, I taught art at a large school. To small children." He was breathless with excitement. Alik turned to Maran, taking her by the shoulders and kissing her. "Something stayed the same, something didn't change." He sighed, smiling, then turned back to his host. "Tamald, will you take me to them, so I can meet them?"

Tamald nodded. "Of course. They will want to see your work. And we must get you a designation badge . . ." His voice faded as he led Alik into the paths of the village.

Darryil the Hunter had taken his band of children to the fields where the verhi roamed. Tamald the Apprentice had taken Alik to find his place. Women sat with their babies and sang as they stitched and wove. Older children gathered outside the schoolhouse, waiting for their teacher. And Maran was left to stand by the First's door flap, alone.

She sighed thoughtfully and sat down on the soft turf, pulling her knees up to her chest. Alik had been correct—the Arakkans had changed. They had gone through quite a reversion, according to his descriptions of thriving cities with thousands of people. Gone were the metal buildings with their electric lights and plumbing, the colorful clothing; replacing them were small plastic and nylon cabins and rough homespun garments. And the hunters—Maran remembered Tamald referring to himself as "a warrior," but yet she knew Alik had stated that Arakkans were a peaceful people. Could this be part of the change too?

"Maran." Prestun's voice brought Maran away from her musings. "The First will see you now." Maran stood and brushed the grass from her pants. As she took the door from him, Prestun stopped her with a question.

"Where is my brother? Has he taken Alik with him?" Maran nodded and waved him in the direction the two men had gone.

Prestun nodded a thank-you and trotted off after him. She watched him for a moment, then entered the home.

20

There was only one room and it was not very large. A low table was at one end; worn pottery hung on the walls. A shelf ran the entire perimeter of the room, lit candles resting on it. In the center of the room was a circle of men, each sitting on a furry rug. At one end of the room was what appeared to be a metal heating unit. A soft orange light came from it.

A wizened old man with cropped gray hair stood, his companions rising with him. They studied her for a few long minutes before leaving Maran alone with their superior. She knew he must be the First.

The man extended his hands and took hers, giving them a gentle squeeze. "Maran, welcome. I am the First, Tarrok Kandek. Please, sit."

Maran did as she was told, folding her legs underneath her. The First smiled.

"You must have many questions, Maran. But first, I have some of my own: How was your journey? Did you sleep well? I hope the stasis left no ill effects." He smiled again, his wrinkled face crinkling more.

Maran swallowed, suddenly feeling very cold. This man had no idea who or what she really was. He thought she was part of the Pod Mission, as Alik had been, but Maran wasn't. How could she tell him?

"First, I must be honest with you." She drew in a deep breath. "I . . . am not from the Pod Mission, I only found Alik. I am . . . was raised as . . . ," she hesitated. "I was raised as a Frathi. I'm in command training at school. I'm going into the Space Corps."

The old man leaned back a bit, gazing levelly at Maran. A gnarled hand ran over weathered lips, dark purple eyes squinted at her. He cocked his head first one way, then the other, as though trying to gain a clearer picture of what she had just stated. Maran was growing increasingly uncomfortable with his silence. She cleared her throat.

"I hope you are not disappointed."

The First shook his head. Slowly, his voice soft, he responded. "No, Maran, I am not disappointed . . . In fact, I am . . . very honored to meet you." He paused, leaning forward. "Maran, do you know who you are?" She shook her head. "You are—were—the Gift."

Maran shook her head again. "I don't understand. I was—"

The First cut her off quickly. "What were you told about your origins?"

"That I was a product of my mother and father, just like everyone else. Why—"

"And what were you told about your father and mother?" His questions were rapid-fire.

"I was raised by my mother but my father, supposedly, was lost in the forest. But I know that's not true. I saw his picture in a book at the temple. And a priest was there, named Parthul. He told us about the other Arakkans, the ones who had survived. Parthul is the only reason we came here."

The First was nodding. "There was a priest at the temple?"

"Yes," Maran replied.

"No one has been to the temple since it was captured by the Shlatlar so long ago. We did not know if anyone had survived. But if you say Parthul lives, he does. Tonight, in darkness' secrecy, I will send Prestun and Tamald with a party of priests to relieve him of his vows." He paused, rubbing his wrinkled chin. "You have been to the temple, though. Good. That will save me some explaining. And you saw . . . the instruments of hate the Shlatlar used? You saw the catalogs of the dead, the endless lists of names?"

Maran nodded, wincing slightly at the memory. "I saw them," she said softly.

He only nodded. Silence hung between them for a moment as he studied her briefly. Then he asked another question. "What were you told about your people? Your history, if you will?"

Maran sighed. She didn't know where he was going with all of this, but she knew she had no choice but to follow. Maran took a deep breath and answered. "Forty years ago the Frathi came to this planet. They were exploring, looking for a new home. Cities were established and thrived; nothing has changed."

He nodded in satisfaction. "And do you believe this, Maran?"

"I'm not sure."

"Would you believe that a whole race of people lied to its children, and to itself?"

"Perhaps."

He leaned back again, recrossing his legs. "What you were told is a lie. Yes, the Frathi were explorers looking for a new home. But that home was already occupied. We offered to share what we had, to be neighbors. But their leader, Commander Dazon, had visions of power and glory; he told his people that because we would not succumb to his will, we were therefore inferior and did not deserve to live. We were to be stricken from this land to make way for the Frathi. Do you believe that, Maran?" He eyed her for a response. Maran sat in stony silence. The First went on with his narrative. "We fought them as well as we could. The war lasted ten years, perhaps a bit less. During that time, entire cities were burned to the ground. Thousands were lost. The Frathi were ruthless. I was but a young man, not many years older than you—How many summers are you, Maran?"

She was startled by the sudden change in direction. "I'm eighteen," she replied, a bit bewildered.

"Hmmm, I guess I was older. Oh, well. No matter. Even I fought with the armies, though we really didn't have a chance against their weapons. But I survived; I was one of the fortunate ones, considering how outmatched we were. They had powerful weapons—guns and laser cannons. We, being peaceful, had only what weapons we could quickly fashion. Some managed to steal from them and use their own arms against them. Several arsenals were captured. It amazes me that we held on as long as we did." He shook his head, temporarily lost in thought. "We called them the Shlatlar, the Destroyers, for wherever they went carnage was left in their wake. They had abandoned their moral values with everything else; their religion, their politics, their original name of Earther Human. Now, they simply called themselves Frathi, meaning "Seeker" in their new language. And their leader left nothing standing in his search for and persecution of us. It was horrible.

"So many were lost, we knew that we would not survive as a race. Although the war itself only lasted ten years, skirmishes went on for another eight years. In the nineteenth year after the Shlatlar landed, we set the Pod Mission in motion, sending the ship into space. But just when we thought we had reached the brink of extinction, we had a stroke of luck—the Shlatlar leader suffered an illness and died. The illness was part of an epidemic that swept their two cities and reduced much of their population. Fortunately, it was native to Arakka, and we were immune.

"Their totalitarian government was thrown into confusion. During that year, the peacemakers of the Frathi, those known as the Andri, raised their voices against those still hungry for war. They had gained popularity as the sickness claimed more lives. You see, the sickness is carried by biting insects. So with the soldiers infected and dying, the Shlatlar leader had fewer forces. Then he himself was infected as he made a 'morale' trip to the battlegrounds. After his death, there was a mutiny among the soldiers who survived. The majority had shifted as the soldiers in the field were infected. One of the Andri was elected leader, in the place of the dead tyrant. We took this opportunity to offer a gift—a child for them to raise as their own, in their own image. This way, in the future when there was more understanding, the child could return to its people and unite us as one. It almost worked."

"What happened?" Maran's voice was a whisper. She almost didn't want to know.

"The infant child was taken into Frathi custody and placed in a respectable home. The woman chosen was unmarried, but an upstanding citizen in the community and a major influence in the Andri peace movement. She took an oath to raise the child in only the kindest fashion and to inflict no harm upon it, nor let it ever come to harm. Both our peoples were happy and we lived in peace. This period of serenity lasted for almost two years. Then their new leader was assassinated.

"The Frathi government was once again plunged into confusion. This time the Shlatlar came out on top. We were not persecuted again as such, but we were driven farther into the forest. We were cut off from the natural resources we had been using to rebuild. We made what we thought was the only logical decision: to return to the old ways of hunting and gathering and living in nature. And so we remain, some twenty years later."

"If the Shlatlar were leading the government, why was I allowed to live?"

The First shook his head. "That I do not know. Perhaps your new mother had grown so attached to you that you were saved for that reason. Perhaps the Shlatlar government feared that killing you would incite an uprising. I do not know the answer. But, regardless, you were spared and have returned to us. We have long been preparing to battle the Shlatlar and regain our home; our only hindrance has been that we do not have someone to unite us, to bring us together as one. And your knowledge of Frathi ways will help us in our combat, help us to predict their moves. Our warriors need someone special to defeat the five thousand Shlatlar troops, to crush a population of twenty-five thousand. You are that someone special, Maran. You can unite us. I feel certain that you have come to help us."

Maran stared at him, stunned. She suddenly remembered the prophecy Alik had told her on their first night together: *"Whoever opens the eyes of the First to Return will lead his people to a new frontier."* She was expected to fulfill it. The prospect was overwhelming. Maran felt herself growing lightheaded at even the thought. The First's face seemed to warp before her eyes and Maran had to look away for a moment. It was impossible. She couldn't shoulder that kind of responsibility.

Tarrok continued, his lined face suddenly becoming that of a young warrior's, hardening with conviction. "Even now they continue to oppress us. Though your mother may hold a position in the government, it is still headed by a Shlatlar. And as long as the Shlatlar are in control, there can be no true peace. You are our only hope, Maran. You must help us."

Maran could only stare at him in stupefied silence. Slowly, she nodded. "I'll try," she finally whispered.

21

Where is Alik?" Prestun had finally discovered his
brother's whereabouts. "Where did you take him?"
Tamald gestured to a dwelling much like all the others. "I
took him to the Artisan Superior. She watched as he painted
and she thought very highly of his work."

Prestun nodded. "She should know. Will she take him on
as an apprentice?"

Tamald smiled, as though he had some hand in the decision. "He is wearing a blue badge," the youth replied by way
of answer. "But what of his companion, Maran? We must find
her a place. It would not do for her to sit with the other women,
and she has more skill than is required to be a seamstress or a
gatherer."

Prestun was thoughtful for a moment. In all of his twenty-
two summers, he had never seen anything like what was oc-
curring now. A sort of energy he had never felt before had
gripped the village. He could see it in the wide eyes of the children as they watched him; he could hear it in the distant calls
of the verhi that roamed in their pasture. It was a physical

thing, and he wished he could understand it.

"Maran is very beautiful." Tamald's declaration was sudden and matter-of-fact.

Prestun laughed, a staccato burst, and cuffed his sibling on the shoulder.

"What?!" Tamald asked, indignant. "What?!"

"Do you really think she would be interested in you, a mere boy? Tamald, my brother, my friend, you dream big dreams. That I must grant you."

"It could happen."

"No," was the laughing response, "no, it won't, I guarantee. She has Alik." He smiled smugly. "I would not be surprised if they had already bonded."

Tamald looked at his brother in shock. "Prestun, there are children near! Watch yourself. Do not make idle accusations like that, when you do not know whether they are true. I may be young, but I know when to hold my tongue—something you have never known."

Prestun glared at his brother, but it soon softened to a smile. "You are right, Tamald. For once."

Diella was angry. People were going behind her back and she hated that. Her fists balled at her sides, she stormed up to the doorway of the home she shared with her father, her black hair flying in the wind she created. Diella didn't bother taking a moment to try to regain some shred of composure. Her anger would be difficult to abate. Shoving the door aside, she entered.

Her father automatically rose, followed by a strange woman. She was lovely, with long hair and big eyes that shone in the light of the candles and the heating unit. Diella noticed the woman's strange clothing, but didn't let it deter her from her purpose in coming.

"Who are the strangers in the village?" She demanded, hands on her hips. "And why wasn't I told? Darryil was not even told. As warriors, we should be notified. You know that, Father."

The First sighed. "Maran, may I present to you my daugh-

ter, Diella." He turned to the young woman. "Diella, this is
Maran, one of the strangers." Briefly, he told her of Maran's
past and her journey with Alik to the village. Maran studied
Diella as the warrior's father spoke, and she noticed the young
woman begin to relax. Of that, Maran was somewhat relieved.
She didn't want to be the cause of a family quarrel.
Diella stood silently, not asking any questions, simply letting her father speak. Idly, her fingers—as though having a will
of their own—played with one of the bead strands attached to
her woven vest that served as a shirt. Her freckled face was the
image of stoicism, with only an occasional gleam of curiosity
squeezing though. Finally, Tarrok completed his recount and
there was silence in the room.

Diella snorted. "I still should have been told. I am almost
a full warrior. I hope you haven't forgotten."

Tarrok smiled patiently at his daughter. "No, I haven't forgotten. You are what I hold most dear, my daughter."

Diella succumbed to a smile, and Maran saw that she was
actually quite pretty. "Well, I suppose I can forgive you." She
smiled and kissed her father on the cheek, then turned to
Maran, looking at her curiously. "Where will she live?"

"There is a vacant house that can be erected near the edge.
Do you know it? I believe Darryil has the house stored near the
meat shed."

"Yes, he does. I'll assign someone to make it ready."

"Meanwhile," Tarrok continued, "please take Maran to see
the Umak'Daahl."

"Yes, Father." She turned to Maran. "This way."

"I've lived here for . . . six summers." Diella paused, thinking.
"That's when we all had to move because the Shlatlar drove us
out again. They do that every so often; it's part of the oppression. You don't realize how fortunate you are, Maran, to have
all the luxuries you do. We have nothing. All we have is our past
and each other, and our past isn't all that wonderful."

"But at least you have a past," Maran said softly. "Until
today, I didn't even have that. I was living a lie and I wasn't

even aware of the fact. You have a family and friends. You have a place in society. You, Diella, are the one who is fortunate, not I."

Diella studied her companion. The afternoon breeze rustled the trees and was gentle on their faces as they walked together to the residence of the Umak'Daahl. The path beneath their feet was as solid as always, but yet Diella had the hazy feeling that she could somehow fall off it if she stepped improperly. Finally, they reached yet another one of the uniform houses and pushed aside the door. Maran entered; Diella did not. But by the time Maran noticed this, she was already inside the house.

The interior was very dark, lit by only one row of candles on the floor. The table was covered in old papers and jars of unknown substances. Dusty books lined the single shelf. Strange shadows danced against the wall, thrown there by the candles. On a fur rug behind the candles, her legs crossed, sat the Umak'Daahl.

"Come closer, child. Sit. Sit." She patted an area next to her on the rug, not even looking up at Maran. "Speak if you wish, but it is not necessary. I already know of your journey and your past." Her voice was deeply accented and slightly raspy. There was an energy that seemed to emanate from her, a palpable force that made the air near her almost quiver. Maran knew that the woman must be very old, but she did not look her years. Her hair was braided and wrapped with a strip of fabric and it hung down her back, nearly touching the floor.

"How do you know?" Maran asked, sitting next to the priestess. Her eyes narrowed suspiciously. "How do you know about me? Who told you?"

Her gaze didn't waver from the fire. "I am Umak; I know."

Maran was becoming uncomfortable with this woman's reticence. She toyed with the hem of her hiking pants. *If she knows all . . .* "May I ask you a question?"

"You may ask me any question, child."

"Did my father die in the forest?"

The Umak paused, almost imperceptibly, but did not look away from the flames. "No, he did not. He was killed in a Shlatlar raid on one of the temples. As was your mother."

Maran was silent. Finally, she knew the truth. Painful though it may be, it was the truth and couldn't be denied. She suddenly felt tired. "I had always wondered," she whispered, "if it was really like they said."

"All truths are open to speculation. In the end, only the facts must remain."

Maran nodded. "How do you know my language?"

This time the Umak's gaze did alter. She turned her face to look into Maran's, her eyes so dark and deep Maran felt she could get lost in them. "All Arakkans have the mindvoice. It is merely a matter of using it. We simply look into that being's mind to their hearts."

"You mean telepathy?" Maran whispered. The Umak was silent. "That's how you knew about me. That's how Prestun and Tamald knew my language. Telepathy." Her eyes were wide as she looked from the Umak's face and into the flames. Her mind was whirling. "Telepathy," she whispered, more to herself than to anyone else.

"Call it what you will. It is the mindvoice, for with it voices can cross the borders of language. With it, there are no borders at all. Each Arakkan has it."

Maran hesitated, thinking. "Do I have it?"

"You are Arakkan. You have the mindvoice. With training, you will learn to use it. Time and training. But you must be patient. For some it comes easier than others. For some, it is very difficult."

"I'll do my best," Maran promised.

The woman nodded, suddenly rising, and walked to the shelf over the table. She took down a bowl of dried fruit and two mugs, pouring water from a bag into them. She returned with her burden to Maran's side.

"It is the Hour of the Second Meal," she said by way of explanation. "We will eat." She took a handful of berries from the bowl, holding them in her palm and one by one placing them into her mouth. Maran ate with her, the sweetness of the fruit dancing across her tongue. For some reason she was reminded of the meals she had shared with Alik; Maran found herself wondering how he was faring.

"Your companion, Aliksandar Pellen. You feel very deeply for him, do you not?" The Umak's eyebrows rose with the query.

Maran nodded. "Yes, we're very close. He is the only person who has made me feel as though I belong. I would do anything for Alik."

"You love him?"

"Yes." Maran said it without hesitation.

The Umak nodded.

"Why do you ask, Umak?"

"There may come a time, Maran, when you must choose between Alik and other circumstances. I cannot say what those circumstances may be, but it will be a difficult decision for you. You must be prepared in your heart and your mind for the difficult times that are ahead of us. You must be ready for what comes."

"But how will I know? How will I choose?"

The Umak shook her head, raising her hand. "Ask me nothing of that, for I am unable to answer. I can only say that you must be prepared. *You must be ready.*"

Maran was silent for a long moment. Questions raced through her mind in random, ricocheting bursts. But one question was most prominent: "Umak, did you know my father?"

The Umak sighed softly. "Not well. We were not of the same order at the temple. But I know that he was a much respected man. He was a powerful priest with a strong mind." She paused, her voice softening. "And he loved your mother very much, Maran."

"My father was a priest?" For some reason, Maran had never really wondered what he had done in life, only whether or not he even existed. Now, to hear about him—it was almost too much joy for Maran to bear.

The Umak nodded, a tiny smile breaking through her stoic facade. "Yes, he was a priest. Almost an Umak. Your mother was a priestess. Teerla did a great amount of work in aiding the refugees that came to the temple to hide. She, too, was much respected." She paused, cocking her head thoughtfully. "As the refugees came in, many were wounded or ill. Some were dying. Your mother, Maran, was key in supervising their care. She also helped keep records of those fallen in the war."

"Those fallen . . . ?" Maran felt herself chill. The book by the altar—it had been a record book of war victims. The scribe that had been notating the names . . . Could she have been . . . Teerla was the name Parthul had said. He had called her Teerla's angel.

"Maran," the Umak said softly, "you have a powerful mind, like your father's. Like your mother's. I believe you will . . . easily learn the mindvoice. I would like to assess your abilities."

" 'Assess my abilities?' " Maran repeated. She was very uneasy. "How?" she asked. "Will it hurt?"

This time a full smile crossed the older woman's face. "No, child, it will not hurt. I will simply lay my hands against your head. You may feel my thoughts and perhaps see images, but there will be no pain. Are you willing?"

Maran looked down at the empty bowl between them. Once, it had been brimming; now, it was vacant. As vacant as she felt. Little by little, her past was being eaten away and replaced by something foreign that Maran barely even recognized. She had to learn to recognize it, though. Maran could not deny the truth.

"I am willing," she whispered.

The Umak nodded. She gently placed her fingertips at Maran's temples, exhaling deeply. "Now, relax your mind, Maran, and do not be afraid. You may see colors or images, but not necessarily. Their clarity will depend on how relaxed you are and your mind's abilities . . ."

The Umak's words faded off as Maran became aware of a tickling sensation on the top of her head. She moved to scratch it, but then realized the feeling was inside her. Colors appeared in her mind—deep oranges, vibrant reds and yellows. A swirl of violet trickled in to solidify and condense.

Maran found herself gazing into a man's dark eyes.

Father, she whispered. But the words were not audible in

reality; they echoed around inside her head, bouncing off her mind's walls. Her inner voice sounded strange and Maran had difficulty believing it was hers. But there was no doubting that the image before her was that of her father. *Father,* she called again. He smiled, his eyes twinkling. As if in slow motion, he raised his hand and offered it to her. Somehow she took it and was enveloped with him in a lavender mist. It swirled and danced around them, and Maran saw faces and images within it. Faces of her friends: Iri, Daken, Wix, and Rheet. Faces of the Arakkans: Tarrok the First, Diella, Tamald, and Prestun. The face of Jinas, the woman who Maran once thought of as her mother. The face of Aliksandar. Each appeared before her and then faded away into the purple fog. Finally only one face remained: her father's.

"Maran," his whisper sounded unexpectedly inside her mind. *"These are your people; you are within them and they are within you. This is your time; run with it. I give you my blessing. Have whatever your heart desires."*

"Father, how will I know what to do?" Maran asked. The words were difficult to form; she knew that the Umak's hold on her must be wavering.

He smiled. *"You will know, my daughter. You will know."* He paused. *"I must show you something. You may not understand it, and you may be afraid, but know that you are safe."*

He gestured for Maran to walk past him and she found herself back in the temple. She was kneeling before the altar, staring down at the name catalog and watching a woman's hand carefully writing in neat script. The woman paused to redip her quill pen, studied the page briefly, then continued the task.

A harsh, explosive noise sounded.

Maran started and blinked.

When she returned her focus to the woman, Maran found her slumped across her book, the back of her skull ruined, blood streaming down her long black hair and onto her face. Her mother's face. Maran raised her hands to her mouth, trying to bottle in a scream; somehow she managed to force it back down her throat. In a strange cloud of detachment, Maran found herself looking into the priestess' face, studying the way her nose sloped and her lips curved, gazing into her wide, death-glassy eyes. *She was beautiful,* Maran thought to herself. She was still staring at the fallen body, watching it and the surrounding scene dissipate and vanish, when Maran felt her father's gentle hand on her shoulder.

"*Your time here has ended; you must return to your reality. Farewell, my beautiful child.*" Even as he spoke, his body began to fade, becoming once again part of the metamorphic swirl of colors. Then, they, too, diminished to be replaced by the wise face of the Umak. Maran blinked herself back into reality as the Umak drew away her wrinkled hands. She was looking hard at Maran, studying her. Slowly, she nodded to herself.

"Your mind, too, is strong. You can see images, though you have had no training." She glanced over at the candles, thoughtfully. "You will go now; I am in need of time to think. Diella will take you to your new home. Good day, Maran."

With that she fell silent, her stare reattaching itself to the fire. Maran sighed. Only a bit less confused, she rose and left the Umak's dwelling.

22

It had all changed.
Alik stared around at the walls of the house he was to share with Maran, the house Prestun had brought him to not long ago. In his world of chaos, the houses were the only things uniform. His was exactly like the Artisan Superior's home, if not a bit smaller. It had the same type of low table, the same kind of plastic floor, the same sort of sleeping pallets rolled up in the corner. He unfurled one of the bedrolls and sat down upon it, facing a row of candles he had lit. Alik unlaced the front of his new vest and took it off, folding it carefully beside him. He closed his eyes and tried to relax.

It had all changed.
Gone were all the buildings, the schools and worship centers and stores, the city halls and offices. Gone were the conveniences of electricity, marketplaces. Gone were the peaceful people he had known. In their place was a race that simply lived to wait and be led in their revenge. It was a race of people with which Alik didn't know if he could live.

They didn't want any part of him, he knew. He was a man

of peace. Even after the war had begun, he had remained true to his beliefs. He wasn't alone then—others felt as he did. But he was alone now. The Arakkans meant well and tried to claim their revenge was in the name of justice, but their anger and hostility toward the Frathi were only thinly disguised. He couldn't ask them to change their ways, and he couldn't change his own. They needed to make peace and compromise with the Frathi, but the Arakkans refused to see the light.

And how long would Maran remain true to the ways of peace? She had been raised by an aggressive, competitive society, and though she claimed to understand his views of peace, he didn't know if she actually believed in them. He hadn't seen her all day, but through his empathic bond with her, he could feel her beginning to change as the Arakkans influenced her, as they turned her to their way of thinking. Alik covered his face with his hands. He was so confused. "Help me," he whispered to the empty room, "someone please help me." Tears began to flow down his cheeks, wetting his palms and wrists. But the tears only lasted a moment. Alik began to quietly recite a prayer of guidance, focusing on the candles, feeling his mind drift from his body.

Maran entered her new home as the sun began to consider its descent into the trees. She stood in the semidarkness for a moment. *Quiet. Everything is so calm, so quiet.* There was a peaceful stillness in the room; Maran let her body absorb the silence.

She saw Aliksandar's form sitting in front of a line of candles much like the Umak had. Instantly she was kneeling by his side, her hand on his shoulder. His eyes were staring unblinkingly at the flames and his mouth moved but no words came out. "Alik?" she whispered, peering at him in the dim light of the candles. "Are you all right?"

His trance broke. "Maran," he whispered.

She saw where he had been crying, even as tears came to his eyes again. "Maran," he whispered, "they've changed. They're not like me. They don't understand me. I'm lost. I'm so lost." Maran put her arms around him and he buried his face against her neck. Gently she stroked his hair and back.

"It's all right," she whispered soothingly. "It's all right, Alik, I'm here. I won't leave."

"I just can't help but feel crushed by all of this," he said softly. "I don't really belong here. I don't know what to do now that I've returned. It's just as I feared—they've grown past me. They changed and I didn't. Maran, I almost wish I hadn't chosen to go on the Pod Mission. I wish I could have died with the masses and that I didn't have to face this. But now I do have to face it." He looked into her eyes. "And I'm so afraid that you will become like them, in trying to help your newfound people. I don't want this to separate us, Maran."

She laid her hand against his cheek. "You won't lose me."

Alik smiled tiredly through the remnants of his tears. "I hope not," he said, gently taking her hand. He shook his head, chuckling softly. "I hope I never lose you." He smiled at her again; trying to forget his depression, he looked into her shining violet eyes. She was so beautiful, her spirit so magnificent— Alik felt fortunate to be with her. She was at the center of his small world. And as long as she stayed there, everything would be all right.

"Don't worry, Alik, it's okay." She kissed his forehead, then kissed his lips. Her hands slid up his chest, her arms encircling his neck as Maran's lips continued to press to his with a passionate intensity she didn't know she possessed. Gently, she pushed him down against the fur mat while she reached for the lace on the front of her new Arakkan vest.

He needs me tonight, she thought to herself, pulling the cord loose. *This is the right time.*

He pushed himself up onto his elbows, hovering over her and kissing her softly. She smiled up at him, her eyes shining brightly. Alik turned onto his side and she snuggled next to him. She sighed, her head against his chest.

"Maran," he whispered after a few moments of silence, "Are you okay?"

She smiled. "Yes," she replied softly. "I feel . . . incredible."

He kissed the top of her head. The fire cast a warm glow into the small room; he was completely at peace. Whatever demons had plagued him earlier were gone for now. All that he felt was a euphoric love that coursed through his veins.

"Maran—"

"Alik—"

They had done it again, spoken in unison. Maran giggled. "I went first last time; it's your turn."

Alik grinned and looked over at the fire. "I have a question for you, Maran. You don't have to answer immediately if you don't want."

"Ask."

He paused, searching for words; he couldn't find them. What he wanted to do was mindvoice his feelings to her, but he wasn't certain if her mind could handle the intensity of what he wanted to say. He knew that in order for his words to be true, the mindvoice was necessary, but he couldn't risk hurting her. She wasn't experienced with mindvoice yet. In the end, Alik opted to simply state it, though words alone could not do justice.

"Maran," he began, "when I am with you, I see a part of my soul that I never knew existed. We . . . are like a single unit. I don't want anything or anyone to come between us and our love."

He paused. Silence hung.

She looked up at him and blinked expectantly. "And?" Maran prompted.

Alik took a deep breath. "And . . . I mean, I was thinking . . . We should always be together. I know we're very intimately involved, but I wanted it to be voiced that we are . . . *ambrie,* together." He immediately looked down at Maran to gauge her reaction.

Maran stared at him a moment, a smile twitching at the corner of her mouth. Slowly, it spread across her face, the firelight dancing in her violet eyes. She slid up him and kissed his lips tenderly, passionately. Alik wrapped his arms around her, holding her close as he shifted his weight and rose up onto his elbow. Maran slowly pulled her lips away, smiling again. She turned onto her back, folding one arm behind her head.

"You're right," she whispered, "we are a single unit. And I . . . I love you like I've never loved anyone. Nothing can tear us apart, Alik."

He smiled, feeling relief and love surge through him. He was hers. She was his. *Always.*

23

Maran had finished dressing when she heard Diella's voice calling from outside the dwelling.

"Maran?" Diella called from behind the door flap. "May I come in?"

"Yes, Diella. Enter."

Diella stepped inside, closing her eyes to let them adjust to the dim light. She opened them as Maran was rolling up the blankets and replacing them in the corner. "Where is Alik?"

"He's off to study with the Artisan Superior. She said that she would take him down to the lake today and they would work on painting a reflection. Apparently it's quite an art, getting the right amount of white pigment and whatever."

"How did you sleep?" Diella asked.

Maran couldn't help grinning. "Just fine."

Diella smirked. She knew that look. She had seen it on her sister's face after her wedding night. If Maran was trying to hide a secret, she was doing an awful job.

"Diella," Maran said in what she hoped was a nonchalant

voice, "what are the Arakkans' customs on having relation-ships, being together?"

Diella's smirk broadened to a grin. "Generally, the man re-quests that he and the woman stay together, live together. It's called asking *ambrie* to someone. After a while, if that works out, he proposes marriage. Did he ask you *ambrie* before or after?"

Maran couldn't believe Diella's nerve, but she decided it didn't matter. She grinned, blushing at the memory. "Before. Pretty much."

The other woman laughed. "Pretty much, eh?" She smiled. "The first step is just to live with him, see how you get along. Although you already do that. Once he actually proposes, the next step is to announce your intentions to the First and the Umak. Then you get married in a ceremony conducted by the heads of the village, my father and the Umak."

Maran nodded.

Diella looked thoughtful. "You'll be told what is expected of you as a married couple, and there will be flowers and feast-ing. You'll have a woven dress; he'll get new clothes. The whole village joins in the celebration."

Maran smiled. "I'm sure it's great." She grinned again, twirling. "I'm just so in love!"

"Maran, I don't want to spoil your fun, but I have some-thing serious to say." Diella paused. "My father talked to the Umak." She sat down on the table, crossing her legs. "She wants you to start training in mindvoice. But Father wants you to train with Darryil in the ways of the warrior. He says he can see the warrior's fire in your eyes."

Maran didn't immediately reply. Her buoyant mood began to diminish as she thought of her promise to the First. He wanted her to unite his people against those that had raised her. She was as much part of the Frathi as she was of the Arakkans, if nothing else then because she was raised as a Frathi. *But to help someone destroy them . . . ?* Maran didn't know if she could do that.

"What do you think I should do, Diella?"

Diella frowned, thoughtfully biting her lip. "I honestly

don't know, Maran. It's your choice. The Frathi are not your people by blood. They destroyed those that are and denied you your heritage. They wanted to exterminate us and they almost did. They lied to you, and to the youth of Frathi society. You would have good reason to hate them. But they did raise you. They did give you a home."

Maran nodded.

"You can do one of three things, Maran," Diella said. "You can bring us together in peace. You can unite us in war. Or, you can altogether refuse to unite us." Diella uncrossed her legs and stood. "It's your decision. But you need to make it soon. Father will want an answer. As will the Umak. You have to decide, Maran."

Maran sighed. She shook her head. "If I unite you in peace, it may not work. We already know that the Frathi—the Shlatlar—don't want equality, they want domination. And I can't just turn my back on my own race. But if I unite you in war, in revenge, I'll lose Alik. I don't want to risk that."

Diella frowned. "Why would you lose Alik?" she asked.

Maran pursed her lips and tried to find a way to explain. "Alik . . . isn't like you and the other Arakkans, Diella. He still believes in the old ways—the ways of peace and negotiation. He cannot accept the new Arakkan philosophies."

"There was a time," Diella said, sighing, "when we were all violent and warlike. Yes, even the Arakkans. It was only after we nearly destroyed ourselves fighting that we were forced to learn the ways of peace. Only then, after much bloodshed and death, were we able to truly progress." She laughed mirthlessly. "Perhaps we learned the lessons of peace *too* well. That was before the Shlatlar came. It was *their* barbarism that nearly destroyed us, Maran. We Arakkans still share brotherly love, but we can't share it with the Shlatlar because they won't accept it. We can't force them to do something they don't want, Maran. Surely you must understand that. All they know is violence. All they want is to oppress us. It is not a question of choosing warfare over peace. There is simply no alternative. If we do not fight, we will be exterminated. Even Alik must accept the truth of this.

"We're tired of being driven into the ground," she said, her voice rising angrily. "You don't know what it's like to fear for your life, Maran. The way the Frathi oppress us is horrible. Whenever they suspect we're beginning to progress, they raid our villages, steal our food, and then burn our villages. Anyone who tries to stop them is killed on the spot. Even children. *Children,* Maran. Murdered. They treat us as one might a rebellious animal. No better. How can you even consider not helping us? How could you be so close-minded? I know you have the warrior spark in you, Maran. You would be an inspiring leader. If only you would agree to lead. Please, Maran, for the children, if nothing else. Please." Diella was looking at her plaintively and Maran couldn't turn away.

"If I'm to be a true leader," she said softly, staring down at her hands, "I'll need both kinds of training—warrior and mind-voice." She looked up at Diella. "Tell your father I accept, but on one condition. I won't command your people. I will not take up a weapon against my own people. I will organize the Arakkans and I will help with strategy. But that is all." She sighed. "I cannot break my promise. No matter how justified the cause might be. I cannot break my promise."

"A promise to Alik, you mean?"

Maran nodded. "I can't lose Alik, Diella. I'm sorry."

Diella stood, and as she exited the dwelling, Maran followed her out onto the short grass. The small village was bustling, women and men crisscrossing each other's paths. Children screeched in their games, chasing each other around houses and dodging the adults that called to them. Maran spotted Darryil talking with Prestun; the latter was gesturing emphatically. Darryil shook his head, sadly. Maran wanted to ask what was wrong, but Diella led her in another direction. Maran watched them for as long as she could before they were obstructed from view.

"And he was dead."

Darryil shook his head. "How did it happen?"

Prestun shrugged. "We found him in a hall. As best as we could discover, the Shlatlar somehow found out about the temple and went to investigate. When they arrived, they found Parthul and killed him."

"Method?"

"Blast to the forehead."

"Then he saw it coming." Darryil shook his head again. Prestun glanced down at the soil. "He was bound and gagged."

Darryil closed his eyes. *That poor old man didn't have a chance. Why did he have to be so loyal to his vows? Why did the Shlatlar have to be so cruel?* Hate welled inside his chest. "Was any damage done to the temple?"

Prestun nodded. "The tapestries had burn marks on them, and some of the wall carvings had been desecrated."

"We should lead a party against them. But I have a feeling it wouldn't do any good." Darryil's jaw worked angrily. He swore under his breath. "That girl, I bet it was that stranger, that girl."

"Maran?"

"Is that her name? Maran. Doesn't even sound Arakkan. And Tarrok wants me to train her. Says he sees the warrior spark in her." He snorted. "She probably found the temple and told her friends in Kalak Lar. She and that man—"

"You mean Alik?"

He nodded. "Their friends then told their government. They found Parthul." He rubbed his chin. "That woman won't bring us anything but bad luck! The First should send her home. Chances are none of her people knew about Alik, so he won't be missed. But she's going to get us killed. Mark my words, Prestun."

Prestun nodded in a vague manner. He didn't know what he should say, if anything. Darryil was obviously too angry to listen. In the end, Prestun made no comment.

Maran stared dumbly at the First. She couldn't believe what she had just been told. Parthul was dead. *How? When? Why?* The questions pummeled her mind. Maran's stomach churned. Parthul was dead. *Parthul was dead.*

"What did you tell your friends about the temple, Maran?"

"Well . . . We all went the first time, the five of us and Alik. He took us, to prove that he was really Arakkan. Then Alik and I decided to go back, just the two of us. But I didn't tell anyone. Really, I—Oh!" Her eyes widened. "Iri . . . Iri called and asked me how I was going to spend my day, and I told her Alik and I were returning to the temple. But she wouldn't have told."

"Perhaps if you had returned home that night. But you've been gone two nights now, Maran. Certainly your friend would've become concerned. And now a priest is dead, a man that spent his life in the service of our god." Tarrok paused. "Do you see now how the Shlatlar work? How they center themselves in violence? Do you see now why we seek to rid Arakka of their hate?"

"But hating them isn't the answer!" Maran said in frustration. "Two wrongs don't make a right!" She wished Alik were there to support her. Maran looked over at Diella, hoping for her voice of sympathy, but the First's daughter remained silent.

Tarrok flew into a rage. "The death won't stop until they are gone! All of them! The attack of the temple was an act of war! We must retaliate and we will do it with or without your help." Tarrok's eyes narrowed into a snarl. "I had high hopes for you, Maran. But you have let me down."

"I never refused to help you," she corrected, her voice dangerously low. "I will join your people, but not in hate. I will not kill blindly."

Tarrok's jaw worked as he stared frigidly at Maran. "Diella, take her to see Darryil. The Shlatlar's blasphemy will not go unpunished."

24

So, you are Maran." Darryil studied her, squinting in the sunlight, its rays glancing off his red badge. "Becoming a warrior takes a great deal of discipline. A great deal of patience. Have you any training at all?"

Maran nodded. "I was in command training at home, in the Frathi community. Part of my courses consisted of battle training. I am experienced with blasters, rifles, and crossbows. I know offensive and defensive techniques. I have some knowledge of verhi riding, but that was pleasure-riding and not combat related."

Darryil nodded, trying not to show that he was impressed. "It doesn't sound like you need much training." He paused. "Nevertheless, I would like to test you."

Maran nodded. "I would expect no less."

He turned to Diella. "Bring me two rifles, a crossbow, and a quiver of arrows." She nodded and strode off in the direction of a small building that Maran supposed was where the weapons were stored. Moments later, she returned, her arms full. After presenting Darryil with the weapons, she returned to the shed to take inventory for the coming battle.

Maran was put through a series of tests. She fired the cross-bow, using all of the arrows allotted her and hitting the target's center with each effort; she was equally skilled with the rifle. Darryil engaged her in an obstacle course on verhi-back and was genuinely surprised when she only felled one of the wooden tubs. For the final test, he challenged her to hand-to-hand combat.

The two circled each other, scanning for weaknesses. Maran feinted toward the right, ducking behind him as he rushed her, catching Darryil's arm and pulling him to the ground in one fluid movement. Immediately shifting her weight, Maran rolled herself on top of him, maneuvering herself into a crouch on his chest. She placed her knee on his throat.

He stared up at her for a long moment. Finally, Darryil spoke. "I cease."

She nodded, accepting his surrender, and stood. She offered her hand to him, but he refused it, standing on his own. She knew he had not expected a quick defeat. And though he had size on his side, she was more agile. He brushed the grass from his vest and breeches, watching Maran all the while.

"Your skills . . . are good. Very well honed. You were trained by an expert, or you are a quick learner, perhaps both. Nevertheless, you are a warrior. I would place your rank at the level of Diella's."

"Isn't Diella about to receive her full warrior rank?" Maran asked. "Is it fair for me to gain rank so quickly when I haven't even trained under you?"

Darryil studied her. "Diella was not chosen by the prophecy to unite us against the Shlatlar. You were. And your training is not complete, Maran. You have yet to master riding. I will place your emphasis there. Our forces will be mounted when the time comes for you to lead us—"

"Warrior Darryil!" someone shouted. A youth ran up to them, panting from exertion. "Please forgive me for interrupting you with your student."

"You have committed no offense. Speak."

The child paused, still trying to catch her breath. The way

she stared at Darryil, Maran could see that the girl considered herself someone special to even be speaking to him. She obviously adored the older man.

"Warrior Darryil, the Umak requests the presence of Student Maran in her dwelling. Immediately." This last word was said somewhat hesitantly, as though the girl was afraid to make a demand she obviously could not enforce herself.

Darryil cast a glance at Maran. "You are excused to see the Umak. I will see you tomorrow morning. You will begin training then." He turned away and picked up the weapons Maran had been using, tucking them under his arm and striding toward the weapons shed. Maran watched him for a moment, then followed the girl to the Umak's home.

The Umak sat exactly where Maran had last seen her, facing the candles, although now there was a second tier. Her legs were crossed in front of her, her hands folded neatly in her lap. She stared unblinking at the fire, even as Maran sat next to her.

"I have been thinking of you." The Umak uttered the statement as though it were of great importance. Maran silently wondered if it really was. She remained quiet, allowing the older woman to continue.

"Your mindvoice is strong. It must be shaped, trained. I will train you, but you must be willing, Maran. You must commit yourself and your time to the training. Do you accept?" She did not look at Maran.

"Yes. I will."

"Close your eyes, child. Tell me what you see, the first image that appears."

Maran closed her eyes. For a moment, she saw only swirls of red and pink, the light from the fire seeping through her eyelids. But then an image did begin to take shape, as the reds darkened and turned to blues and violets. A man stepped out of the blur of shadows.

She had expected to see her father again. "I see Alik," Maran whispered.

The Umak nodded, though Maran couldn't see her. "He

is your center. Your world revolves around him. This is true?"

"Yes."

"Maran, he does not know of your strength with the mind-voice. You must show him, but only when the time is proper. Do not rush. And you must remember that even though you do love him, sometimes people cannot be held together and must go their own ways."

Maran opened her eyes. "I would never leave Alik." Her tone was just less than defiant.

The Umak did not immediately respond. Slowly she looked away from the dancing flames. You and he are different, Maran. You are of the same people, yes, but you are not of the same world. His is gone; yours is beginning. You must do what you believe is correct, even though he may try to stop you. Do what you believe."

Maran stared in bewildered silence at the Umak. She didn't understand. *Why was the woman talking like this? What was going to happen that would make Maran have to choose between her love for Alik and . . . something else?*

"Why are you telling me this?" she demanded of the Umak.

The older woman gazed at Maran reflectively. After a pause, she said: "You are both alike in many ways. Both young. Both confused. Both without a true home. He has found his with you. But yours you must find on your own. His love for you runs deep, so deep sometimes that it almost overpowers him. Every moment of his life is spent thinking of you."

"Yes, I know," Maran replied.

"Has he asked *ambrie* of you?" The Umak's question was abrupt.

Startled momentarily, Maran looked down at her own folded hands. "Yes," she answered truthfully. Boldly. "This morning. Or rather, last night." She let the sweet memory of their togetherness take shape in her mind. And even though she knew that the Umak could probably see into her, could see the image, she wasn't ashamed. It didn't matter. She knew that it was beautiful.

"You must show him your mindvoice, Maran. It is only fair. That is the way in Arakkan society. Anything else would be misleading him. *Ambrie* is a state of great emotion, great unity. Did he show you his mindvoice?" Maran shook her head in reply, and the old woman nodded knowingly.

"He must have been afraid he would overpower you," she explained. "You must tell him of your mindvoice, Maran. Only after you have shared it with him, and he shared his, can you be truly *ambrie*. All that is left then is for him to ask marriage of you. That will come later. For now, you must tell him truthfully how you feel."

"If I unite your people in battle," Maran objected, framing her predicament, "I'll lose Alik. And if I lose him, then I'll destroy our being *ambrie*." Maran said it abruptly. She had to get it off her tongue, out of her head.

The Umak nodded. "Yes, you will. Perhaps. His ways are not the ways of war, of seeking revenge. But these people need a strong leader, Maran, and you are the chosen one. To not unite us would be a greater crime, for it would be finalizing our state of oppression and there would be no chance for us to break free. You must unite us, Maran. Alik will understand what you have to do. He will."

"I can't," she whispered. "I can't lose him."

"Do you believe that he will stop loving you if you unite our people?"

Maran nodded. "He hasn't said as much, but it would greatly disappoint him. I don't want to hurt him. I love him too much to see him hurt." Maran sensed that she was sounding childish to the Umak, whiny and complaining. But she could not deny the truth in her heart. "I don't want to be the chosen one," she decided. "I don't want to be a leader of a war."

The Umak folded, then unfolded her hands. "The Shlatlar invaded the temple and killed a priest," she explained to Maran. "They will be upon the city soon. As we speak they are raising their armies, telling them of the savages in the woods. Before, only the older officers were involved in the raids, remnants from the old wars." Her eyes grew dark and brooding. "Now the young ones will come, too. Young soldiers hungry to prove themselves. Hungry to kill. To kill *your* people, Maran."

"No," Maran said. "Not my people."

"Yes!" the Umak scolded. "The Arakkans *are* your people. And now the enemy soldiers come. They have leaders, but we do not. We will be crushed beneath them. This time there will be no exile. The Shlatlar have had enough of us. I will die; you will die. Alik will die. They will kill us all."

"Maran," she asked, leaning forward, "what if you were to survive? Will you be able to live knowing of the death around you? Will you be able to sleep knowing that children were murdered because you chose to ignore the prophecy? You must choose, Maran. Fight and perhaps live, or walk away, and condemn us all—including Alik—to death."

"I don't know what to do." Her voice was a shaky whisper. Tears welled in Maran's eyes. The Umak was right—she could not let these people die. The Frathi army was much stronger than the Arakkan. It would be a miracle if the Frathi could be beaten. Without a trained leader, it would be suicide. They had to try.

"You must let your soul decide, Maran. Think on it and let your soul decide." She paused. "The time has come for you to leave. I will see you tomorrow." She fell silent. After a few moments of sniffling, Maran regained enough composure to walk through the approaching darkness back to her home.

"Artisan Superior, I have something I need to discuss with you." Alik peered over the stretcher frame that held the fabric he was painting. The old woman across from him raised her eyes from the pigment-mixing bowls and gazed steadily at him. Alik continued: "It's about Maran." He paused, waiting for an answer. None was forthcoming. "I love her so much, Superior, but I can't seem to really tell her. And I just know she's going to be talked into uniting the army and she'll change, and then I'll lose her to the hate that seems to run though the veins of these people. I have nothing without her. I'm a shell without her. That's why I can't stand the thought of losing her to the hate, to the warriors. And I don't know what to do about any of it. And I'm not sure how far . . . gone . . . she is. How much they have won her convictions. She's young, she's easily swayed."

The Artisan Superior nodded. "Have you asked her *ambrie*?"

He nodded.

"Then how can you say you are not certain what she feels? Did you show her your mindvoice?"

"No."

"Why?"

Alik let the question hang in the air while he searched for his answer. "I wasn't certain if she even knew of the mindvoice. She's never used hers, and I didn't want to hurt her."

The Artisan Superior sighed, shaking her head gently and laying down the mixing bone. "You fear hurting her and she fears hurting you."

"She fears hurting me?" Alik was bewildered by the statement.

The woman smiled. "Yes, she does. Maran believes that if she leads in battle, she will hurt you. She thinks she'll lose you, that you will cease to love her. Is this true?"

"War is against everything I believe! We have to make peace with the Shlatlar, not war. I'm not saying surrender, and I'm not saying we should just lie down and take whatever comes. We have to talk. We don't even know why they hate us!"

"The priest at the temple was found dead."

"Parthul?" gasped Alik.

She nodded. "Parthul. He was found tied up, shot in the forehead." She glanced down at the mixing bone, toyed with it a moment before continuing. "The time for appeasement is over. War is inevitable. The warriors will not rest until the Shlatlar blasphemy is revenged. The First will not relent until the Shlatlar threat is gone. They will march. Victory, of course, is uncertain. They are so many and we, well . . . We are few. But the odds of winning are greater if Maran unites them."

Alik stiffened at the suggestion. Slowly, as the truth of the Artisan Superior's words warmed him, his icy resistance thawed. "But does she have the power?" he asked. "Will she know what to do?"

"Tahar will give her the power. And she will find it within

herself. Let her, Alik. Let her find what she seeks—herself."

Alik sighed. "I wish I could find myself."

The Artisan Superior smiled. "You will find what you seek when your spirit is content. That is all I can say. You must discover the rest."

Alik nodded, rolling up the fabric he had painted, and bidded farewell to his teacher. He tied the bundle with a cord, tucked it under his arm. The sun was setting as Alik left the Artisan Superior's dwelling.

Tamald pulled the blanket up around his chest, lying down on the pallet across the room from his brother. They had lived together for two years, ever since their parents had been killed in a raid on the village. The people had been caught unaware and hadn't time to defend themselves. Many were left without parents, like Tamald and Prestun. Not all were lucky enough to be of an age that they could take care of themselves. The younger orphans were adopted into other families; the older were given homes of their own. Now Tamald lay in the darkness, thinking of what was about to happen.

He had never been in a battle. He had been in training courses, but that hadn't been real. This was real. Frighteningly real. People would die.

Tamald glanced over at his brother's silent form. Prestun's back was to Tamald, and he had his covers drawn up to his shoulders. Tamald listened to the rising and falling of his breath. Tamald tried to imagine what would happen to him if his brother was killed in battle. Life as he knew it would end, he decided. He had no idea what he would do without Prestun.

"Are you asleep?" Tamald whispered, propping himself up on his elbow.

"Mmmfff?"

"Prestun, I am troubled. I need to talk."

A loud sigh issued from Prestun and he rolled over onto his back. "What's wrong?" he asked groggily.

"Do you think we will go to battle?" Tamald asked the question bluntly.

Prestun looked over at his younger brother. The door had been propped open for ventilation, and the light from the twin moons played on the youth's worried features, faintly glowing across his cheeks and in his black hair. The elders often told Prestun how much Tamald looked like his father. Prestun didn't remember; he had blocked his parents' faces from memory after their deaths. They were dead. Murdered by the Shlatlar. Remembering them would only be a burden. But every so often he did remember: the raid, the anguish, the pain, the mourning cries from the mouths of the wounded and dying. From his own mouth. He wanted no more raids. No more pain. The Shlatlar would pay for what they had done to his people. They would pay for the terror. They would pay for the blasphemous act of killing a priest. And his parents. He would make sure of that.

"We will go to battle, Tamald, you can rest assured. A week ago, I may have answered differently. The killing of the priest was the final straw."

"Will we go under Maran's lead?"

Prestun pondered the question for a moment. "Whether Maran unites us or not, we are going to battle. Frankly, I suspect that the First is just using her and the prophecy as an excuse to finally unite against the Shlatlar."

Tamald paused, considering what his brother had just said. Was it possible that Maran was simply being used as a figurehead? Would the First do that? It was true that he had been waiting a long time for someone strong to unite the Arakkan villages spread throughout the land. But was Maran that strength? he wondered. Tamald asked his brother's opinion.

"I would be hesitant to say that she is a strength militarily," Prestun replied slowly. "However, she is a very strong woman, mentally. The mindvoice is strong in her. I have heard a story about Maran. The power that had drawn her to the temple, the calling beacon that drew Aliksandar's pod home, was so strong within her that it actually drew in her mindvoice, separating it from her body. I have also heard that she is the product of two from the Holy Order. That alone invests in her a special power.

If anyone can unite a people, it will be one with a strong mind-voice like Maran's."

Tamald nodded. "I do not believe she will unite us, Prestun. She will not risk losing Alik."

Prestun snorted. "She must. She loses him or she loses us. All of us. She must choose soon." Prestun smiled at his worried brother. "Go to sleep. Tomorrow will bring answers, I am certain of it. Good night, my brother."

25

Maran slid under the blankets, laying down and leaning against Aliksandar's back. He was asleep already, his breath soft. He had told her that he couldn't imagine life without her. That he didn't want her to change. But she had changed.

Maran found herself wondering when it had happened. Was it when she was speaking with Diella this morning? Was it something that the First or the Umak had said that had made her see things differently? Or had it been the knowledge that a people could be so cruel as to murder a priest? That was it. Parthul's death. Combined with everything else, *that* was what had made her mind see things in another light. The blood red light of war.

Tears welled in her eyes. The people of this village, and of others she was sure, had nothing but each other—just as Diella had said. Nothing but each other and fear. They were depending on her. She wanted them to make peace, just as Alik did. But they were beyond peacemaking. Nothing would stop them from going into battle. They would lose without her, that much was certain. But she wasn't so sure that they would win with her.

Maran suddenly remembered a time when she was twelve years old and had been in a fight. A boy in her class had stolen her lunch, and Maran had belted him across the mouth. She had felt terribly guilty afterward, but Iri had insisted that she had done the right thing, that now he wouldn't steal from anyone else. The incident seemed quite trivial compared to the situation she currently faced, but Iri's words came drifting back to Maran's mind: *"Maran, don't let your conscience overcome reason."* That admonition seemed oddly appropriate now.

Maran knew what she had to do. She knew also that her decision would crush Alik. But Maran had an obligation to fulfill. What she wanted didn't matter; the safety of a race of people did.

The tears slid down her cheeks, angling off to slip into her ears. She buried her face in Alik's broad, freckled back, shaking in her sobs. *I never wanted this. I never wanted to hurt him. Gods, don't make me do this. Don't make me have to tell him my choice.*

Alik stirred next to her, slowly turning over and onto his side. "Maran, what's wrong? Why are you crying? Has someone hurt you?" His forehead was creased with concern, though his voice was still clouded with sleep.

Maran sniffled and tried in vain to stop her tears. She sat up, pulling the blanket up around her chest. "Alik, I never want to lose you, but I have to tell you something. I want you to know that it was so hard for me to make this decision."

Alik sat up too, staring at her. His voice was very soft. "What is it?" he asked, even though he was afraid that he already knew.

Maran struggled for words. She stared down at her hands, squeezing them closed around clumps of fabric. "I have to do it. I have to save these people. If I don't, the Shlatlar will attack and we'll be defenseless. Alik, I can't let them die. What I need doesn't matter."

"You would help people kill each other? That's what you would be doing." His words were spoken in a soft tone, but their edges were jagged, cutting.

Maran's tears increased. "Alik, don't do this. It's not just my battle, it's yours too. These are your people also. Please . . ."

His face hardened. "Maran, I thought you understood me. That I would never hurt anyone. Maran, I don't believe in vengeance. I don't believe in hate. And there was a time when all Arakkans were like me. The Shlatlar didn't just kill our people, they killed our faith. We lived the word of Tahar. We didn't just believe in it, we *lived* it. It was only with severe deliberation by a council of Umaks that we even fought back against the Shlatlar. But we only fought with the hope that someday we could stop fighting and start negotiating and compromising.

"And I cannot believe that you would choose to kill those that raised you. Like it or not, they are your people. You may be Arakkan by blood, but you are Frathi in all other respects. You mustn't forget that. We should try to find peace, Maran. Our races can be united, I know it."

She shook her head. "I tried to tell the First that peace is the answer, but he wouldn't listen. He says they won't hear our language, that the words of war are all that they know. Alik, if I don't unite the Arakkans, they'll go into battle without any order at all. It will be like condoning a genocide. They'll die for certain then. All I'm doing is helping them to defend themselves. Certainly you can see the logic of that?" She looked at him pleadingly.

"And you think you can organize them. You think that they will follow you." He sighed. "Then do it. I don't know you anymore, Maran. I don't even know myself. But I know one thing."

"What?"

"It saddens me greatly that you have chosen this path. Very greatly."

This time Maran didn't even try to hold her tears in check. They spilled down her cheeks like waterfalls, reddening her eyes. She had felt their love die. It curled within her, like burning paper, withering at the edges and blackening until only ashes were left. Maran was alone. She was surrounded by people that needed her, but Maran was completely alone. She longed to take back what she had just said, but she couldn't. The Umak was right; she'd had to chose between Alik and the battle. Maran hadn't wanted to choose, she wanted both. But that was impossible. The past couldn't be withdrawn, she wouldn't be forgiven. She couldn't forgive herself.

Alik stared at her a moment before lying back down. "It's too late, Maran," he whispered. "I've said all I have to say." His words had an air of finality. Maran shuddered. She lay down next to him, and his body seemed cold against hers. She wouldn't blame him if he never wanted to see her again. They had been like a single body; now, they were torn apart. She had disappointed him, she knew, and there was nothing she could do to rectify the situation. She had hurt him. Maran turned on her side, away from Aliksandar's back. Tears continued to flow down her cheeks even as she slid into sleep's abyss.

I am dead, Alik thought as he heard her sobs fade. Without Maran he was nothing. No one. His life had ended and he was alone. He couldn't continue to truly love her knowing that she was helping to kill. It was against everything he knew. But *could* he really ask her to sit back while a leaderless Arakkan army blundered into battle against a superior enemy? Knowing also that defeat was almost guaranteed without her symbolic leadership? Leadership that had been ordained through prophecy?

A thought slammed into him: *We'll be killed either way.* It was a no-win situation. If Maran refused to lead the army they would be crushed. Their resistance would be too disorganized to be effective. If Maran led them, however, they would still be crushed, just because they hadn't the weapons and sophistication of the Frathi army. It was a no-win situation.

His mind was a hopeless tangle.

Which would be better, he asked himself, allowing Maran to do what he deplored but supporting her decision, or remaining faithful to his beliefs, knowing that he was hurting her? Could he stand by her? But that would mean that he was endorsing this war, and endorsing the human slaughter that would be an inevitable result. Was there greater good in dying to defend oneself—even if that means betraying one's beliefs—or dying in defense of principles?

Alik stared into the darkness. Images of battles and war flitted through his mind. Images of desperate futility. Senseless carnage.

But could Maran be right? What if perhaps, just perhaps, he was wrong . . .

I V

▲

THE
RETURN

26

In the weeks that followed, Maran completed her training for the upcoming battle. She proved to be a quick study and easily mastered riding. Though she was not fully fluent with her mindvoice, she had enough experience for the Umak to approve and release her from intense training. Maran met the First's requirements. As far as he was concerned, they would go to battle in good hands.

But to Maran, those weeks were spent in an unfeeling fog. Ever since discussing her fateful choice with Alik, the two had become distanced. When Alik wasn't busy painting with the Artisan Superior, he spent his time lost in thought or meditating in a trance. Maran knew that his training had ended and that he only continued to use the Superior's home as some sort of refuge. To be away from her, she realized. She had also seen him riding out on the plains alone, his painting supplies strapped to the back of his verhi. He would stay out for hours, sometimes not returning until deep into the night, after Maran had already fallen asleep.

She didn't think that his distance was entirely related to her.

He seemed to be at odds with himself also. It was as if he was fighting some inner war. He was withdrawn and unusually quiet. When they were together, which was rare, he would either stare unseeing at her, or avoid looking at her at all. They spoke little, if at all. And when they did talk, it was only to exchange the briefest familiarities.

Their love, which had been so alive, was truly dead.

Maran longed to try to make things right, to have him take her back. She lay awake at night, next to him yet so far, wishing that he would take her into his arms, that he would love her like he used to do. Maran could close her eyes and feel his arms around her, his flesh against hers, could feel their souls together. And she would grow so frustrated at not being able to have him, at having only the memories, that she would cry, hugging her knees to her chest.

Her world became one of solitude. It was as if she was slowly letting go of herself, the person she was. But who, or what, had she become? Maran wasn't even sure anymore. She felt herself growing more and more like the other Arakkans as they trained her in their warlike ways. She saw the children playing between the houses and thought only of how she would stop the Shlatlar from killing them. That was the only way she could justify leading this war—saving the children from certain doom.

The day after Maran's decision, Prestun and Tamald had been sent with a group of warriors to the other villages. Their mission was to unite all the villages and bring back their forces to add to their own. Maran was surprised to learn that there were so many Arakkan villages. So many, in fact, that each each had been given a name. The one she lived in was called Daar Nakl; the other closest village was Daar Bassl, many miles away over the plains. Their people were greater in number than those of Daar Nakl, so their forces—together—would more than double the army from Daar Nakl. But why so many villages? she asked. And why so far apart?

There had been a strategic plan in creating many small villages instead of one large city.

"If you lived in one large city," Diella had explained, "then when you were attacked all of your people would be at risk.

Correct? By breaking into smaller villages, we have a stronger chance of survival. If Daar Nakl is destroyed, the other villages will survive and our race will survive."

Maran scolded herself for her blunder. "Of course," she admitted sheepishly. It had been a very sensible decision.

The young warriors had arrived home yesterday morning, a slew of fighters in tow. The First had conducted a careful head count and came to the total of eighteen hundred able-bodied warrior men and women that had gathered from the many Arakkan villages. Some villages had sent more warriors than others; the villages were of different sizes and therefore had different capabilities. But each had sent as many warriors as they could. Temporary housing had been set up in and around the village of Daar Nakl and many of the warriors had taken up residence with local families.

Maran had been asked to make a speech to the gathered warriors, something to bring them together on the morning after their arrival. She chose her words carefully, rolling them over in her mind as she approached the First's home. Along with the swollen mass of warriors, the whole of Daar Nakl had gathered to hear her. As she meandered through the crowd a great humming of excitement rippled through them like water. They lifted her upon their shoulders, pushing her up onto the First's roof, the position from which she had been asked to speak.

Maran looked out over the crowd. She searched for Alik, but he was nowhere to be seen. Despite her own apprehension at the enormity of the task before her, she felt her heart sink with disappointment. Where was he, she wondered. What was he thinking about her right now? How upset with her must he be at this moment? Instead of Alik's gentle, reassuring smile, she saw faces of men and women tilted upward, staring expectantly at her, hoping, willing her to ensure victory. She was supposed to promise them something that she wasn't even sure she could deliver. It was impossible. But she had to try. Maran had come too far let them down now.

"My fellow Arakkans," she began in a quavering voice. She faltered. Was this the voice of a leader? She swallowed hard, and began again. "My fellow Arakkans. We are gathered here on this day for a common purpose—to bring a halt to the Shlatlar terror. This can only be done in one way, and that way is cooperation. I know you are all from different villages, and perhaps you do not all think alike, but you must remember that we all fight for the same purpose, and that is to ensure the safety of generations to come.

"I will unite you!" she sang out, and a cheer erupted from the people. "But you must be willing to work together. I feel very strongly that our forces will be effective against the Shlatlar. They must be. The price to be paid for defeat is high! We cannot afford to lose. Each of you, warriors and citizens, must do your best to further the cause and to help in any way that you can. I thank the kind families who have opened their homes to the visiting soldiers; without your hospitality, the war effort cannot be successful. I thank the warriors themselves for coming to Daar Nakl and agreeing to let me unite them against our common enemy, the Shlatlar.

"For it is because of the Shlatlar that we have been forced to divide ourselves among many villages. It is the Shlatlar that has forced us to stay small and stay hidden in order to survive. We came to them in peace; they greeted us with hatred and distrust. We welcomed them with open arms. They drove us from our homes and forced us to live like soulless savages. No longer, my friends. Together, united as one, we will rise up and defeat the Shlatlar. We will show them our might. We will prove to them that we are not simple people who must accept their oppression like common animals. We are intelligent beings, and we have the right to live and think in freedom, as we choose, without fear of punishment from anyone. United we can stop them!"

The crowd thundered its approval, hundreds of fists rising into the air, pummelling it, raised and raised again as the people began to chant over and over: "Kill the Shlatlar! Kill the Shlatlar!"

Maran stared out at them, finding herself nodding. It was then that she noticed a figure making its way through the masses to reach the front of the crowd. Before Maran knew what was happening, several young warriors had lifted him up onto their shoulders and pushed him onto the roof with her.

Maran and Alik stood side by side, but never did they feel more apart.

Alik straightened and looked down at the people. They had become quiet again, confused at the appearance of this new speaker. He watched the puzzled faces for a few seconds, forming his thoughts into words. Better to start at the beginning, he decided. He took a deep breath.

"My name is Aliksandar Pellan," he said. "I am not like you. I lived many years ago, when the Shlatlar first invaded. Yes, I know they killed our people and I recall the pain. I lost my family. I lost many of my friends." He paused, struggling with his composure. "I was chosen for the Pod Mission." From the crowd came a smattering of hisses. Alik raised his hand appealingly. "I know many people thought that the Pod Mission was an act of cowardice, that rather than stand and fight the Shlatlar we were running away. That is not true. We were trying to prevent full-scale genocide in a war that we were destined to lose. I wanted peace among the Arakkans and Frathi, and I agreed to participate in the mission in the hope that when the pods returned we could help establish a new society dedicated to peaceful cooperation. I know how hard we tried to make them see peace." Alik shook his head slowly, then lifted his voice. "I still believe in peace! War will bring destruction to both sides. We will not escape unscathed."

"No!" the shouts rang out.

"Yes!" Alik assured them. "Remember my words when you see heaps of Frathi children lying dead in the streets. Remember my words when you hear the cries of the Frathi mothers mourning their fallen children, their fallen husbands, brothers, fathers. Remember what I've said when you look up at the sky and see smoke from the flames of destruction, when you smell the stench of death, when you hear the anguish of the dying all around you. If we win—*if* we win—the victory will not be without its losses. We will lose too. We will lose by proving to the Shlatlar that our ways are no better than theirs! We will prove that we are no better than the Shlatlar! We will be the same." He paused, breathing heavily, his face red from emotion, his eyes fire. The crowd had grown restless and uncertain.

"Once," he cried out, "Maran and I were in love." The crowd hushed immediately, and Alik's voice grew wistful. "We were *ambrie*. Now, that love has been torn apart by you people. I am ashamed to be called Arakkan, for the Arakkans I knew would never behave like this. We *didn't* believe in violence, we *didn't* believe in vengeance, and we *didn't* believe in hate. We were *peaceful!*" He shouted the word with a force—a passion—that Maran had never seen in him. "We can be peaceful again." Alik tried to calm himself. He sighed wearily. "But you have made up your minds and will not hear me, I know. I won't waste your time any further." He walked to the roof's edge and was lowered into the crowd.

Maran tried to track him for a moment, but he was immediately swallowed by the surging mass of bodies. They turned their eyes back to her, their leader. She stared down at them, suddenly uncertain. "What do you think of Aliksandar's ideas? Shall we try to make peace with the Shlatlar? Shall we try to give this peace an opportunity?" She opened her arms to the crowd, waiting for a response.

The response was resounding: "Kill the Shlatlar! Kill the Shlatlar! Kill the Shlatlar!"

Maran had won. But in her eyes there was not a hint of triumph.

Maran had instructed each of the warrior-delegates to take the name of his or her village to represent themselves; it helped keep their origins clear and, Maron believed, would help maintain morale. The problem, as she was quick to discover, was that each clan jealously insisted that the battle be run his or her own way. It would require all the powers of persuasion Maran could summon—and then some—to convince the feuding clans that they must all fight together.

"We must take their forces head-on!" The warrior-delegate from Daar Bassl, Vasex, thumped his fist on the map spread over the table. Maran flinched, not for the first time. "We cannot wait for them to march on us; we must march on them!"

"Vasex, you fool, you would get us all killed. Stop speaking this nonsense and start using your brain." The warrior Baglu shook her head. "We can't march against them. It's too far for our army; we would be exhausted by the time we reached Kalak Lar."

"How do we know that is where they will concentrate their forces?" Zaepho glanced over at Maran, violet eyes narrowed in his aging face. "They have two cities; Kalak Lar is the smaller of the two. Why would they concentrate there?"

Maran looked down at the map. She placed her finger on the city, as if trying to place it in her mind. *Kalak Lar*, she whispered to herself. It was the town where she had grown up. Where she had been schooled. Where her friends lived . . . Her friends. Maran wondered what had happened to them. Iri, Rheet, Daken, and Wix, what had happened to them all? It seemed like years since she had last seen their faces, yet it was only a matter of months, perhaps not even that long. Maran wondered if they would even recognize her in her rough clothes. Her face was streaked with battle paint. It lined her cheeks and forehead as it lined the other warriors around her. The battle would be soon. She could feel it.

Maran refocused her attention on the map, trying to ignore the gnawing of dread that pulled at her shoulders and gripped the back of her neck.

"Here," Maran said finally, tapping the map. "They'll concentrate their forces near Kalak Lar because Kalak Singh is farther away and it is right on the beach, on a narrow peninsula. They wouldn't take the chance of having their backs to the water if we attack them, which they expect us to do. Baglu is correct, we can't march against them. That would take us nine hours. We would be exhausted from the march and in no condition to fight. Also, we would be too far away to maintain our supply lines." She shook her head. "We have to wait for them to come to us. If we keep them on the move, it will gradually weaken their forces. Also, they aren't familiar with the forest;

they'll be subject to sinkholes and bogs. Men will be lost there, besides those who will be lost in battle. We can only hope it'll be enough to lessen the threat."

"But how long must we wait for the Shlatlar to attack? And what of the citizens? Where will they go?" the warrior from Daar Bassl asked, leaning on the map table.

Maran considered the woman's words. She noticed Darryil, her second in command, studying her, waiting for her response. "I'm not sure when they will come, but I know it will be soon." Maran did not mention that Iri had probably reported her missing and that a search party most likely had found their tracks and then followed them to the village. Undoubtedly the search party had been scouting their defenses under cover of darkness. "We have to get the citizens out of Daar Nakl. But where to take them . . ." She studied the map intently, as though it might suddenly speak and solve her problems. Maran laid her finger on the nearby plateau. "Are there caves in these cliffs?"

Darryil nodded. "But we'll have to cross the river. And with all the rain, it will be an unsafe journey."

Maran looked up from her study of the cliffs. "I know that. But we have boats, and the Arakkans are experienced with the surrounding rivers in ways that the Shlatlar aren't. Plus, the Shlatlar will not expect us to attempt a river crossing like this."

From the assembled warriors there was a murmur of consent. *Good,* thought Maran. *We have at least agreed about something.*

"Our people will be safe hiding in the caves," Maran assured them, "and the rivers surrounding them will provide protection against invaders. Meanwhile"—she moved her finger to another position—"we'll pull completely out of Daar Nakl and wait for them up here, on the plains above the lake."

Darryil saw her line of thinking and began to nod even as Vasex spoke, gesturing to the chart. "We can make a special mixture of peat and wood and pack it into hollowed logs. The firelogs will burn but won't extinguish. We can roll them down on the oncoming troops. Once we have them in retreat, we could effectively pin them against the lake. From there, it would be easy to finish the job."

Maran agreed. "Fire logs, yes. Vasex, you and Baglu are in charge of constructing them." The warriors nodded at Maran as she continued. "We'll also use double envelopment. When they charge our line of warriors, we soften in the middle, giving them false confidence. Then we spread out and surround them, hemming them into the center. They'll be crushed.

"After we have their ranks lessened, part of our forces will split off and march to Kalak Lar. You will secure the city and then proceed on to Kalak Singh. There you may encounter some resistance, since it is a larger city. Just remember that they are against the ocean and can be trapped. After the battle is finished, the Arakkans will remain in the Shlatlar cities.

"Each of you will lead your own village troops. They know you best. But watch for signals from me or Darryil. In the event that something happens to me, Darryil will take command, followed by Diella. Are there any questions?" No one spoke. Maran nodded. "Then let's get to work. We don't have long—"

Maran was cut off by a sudden commotion outside the dwelling. The door was flung open and Tamald thrust his head through.

"Maran!" he gasped. "The First . . . He wishes to speak with you. We have . . . " He paused, still out of breath. "We've captured four Shlatlar soldiers coming here from the temple. He wishes you to be present when he interrogates them. Come quickly." Without another word, Tamald vanished.

Maran stared after him a moment, too stunned to speak. *Four Shlatlar soldiers,* Maran thought. *Could it be?* "Excuse me," she murmured, making her way through the delegates and leaving the building.

27

The four prisoners stood against the wall of the First's home in the center of the village. Their wrists were bound—and curious Arakkans had gathered around them to stare at the two men and two women. Their faces were scratched and bruised from the capture and smeared with dirt. The immaculate white uniforms that they had worn proudly were torn and stained beyond repair. They made a shabby quartet.

As Maran approached the town center and the First's home, she spied Alik threading his way through the crowd, heading in the same direction. He didn't see her, or if he did, he gave no sign. Maran wondered what interest he had in the prisoners. *Perhaps he was simply curious,* she decided, *like all the rest.* Strangely, Maran was disturbed by his presence here. Perhaps some part of her wished that he wouldn't be watching her when she spoke to them. That he would not bear witness to this spectacle. She didn't need his eyes boring holes of guilt into her soul.

"Maran," the First's voice rang in her ears. He stepped out

of the crowd, taking her arm and leading her into the circle cleared around his dwelling. "I wanted you to be here when I question the captive. I wanted you here when I sentence them."

It was then that Maran saw their faces. Her worst fears were confirmed. Maran felt her heart sink as her four childhood friends stared back at her in confused silence.

"Sentence us? What do you mean?" Iri's voice rose in pitch as panic trickled into her blood. "What kind of sentence?" She glanced around nervously at the crowd.

The First cocked his head and grinned smugly. It was clear to Maran that he was enjoying their discomfort. "Whatever type sentence I deem necessary. What were you doing in the forest?"

"We were enlisted by the army," Rheet explained. "Drafted, if you will, for the battle. The four of us, I along with Iri, Daken, and Wix." She gestured to her companions. "We were all posted at the temple—"

"The temple!" shouted someone from the crowd. "What have you done to the temple, you Shlatlar slime?!"

Maran tried to look away, but could not. Her mind was in a torment. She could feel the eyes of her friends on her, pleading with her to do something.

Rheet fidgeted nervously with the only remaining button on her cuff. "It's been commissioned as an outpost. We were stationed there, but we sneaked away to try to find Maran. A tracking party had been sent out to find you, Maran. You had been reported missing, and Iri told them about the temple, and they found your tracks from there to the river . . . and from the river, they found the village. That's why a squadron was posted at the temple, as a sort of halfway point. So, we thought you might be here." She looked at Maran. "Maran, come back to us. There's still a chance for you to be accepted, and they might not punish you for betraying your people."

"When we attack, Maran, you'll be killed," Daken said worriedly. "We don't want you to die. I wouldn't be able to live with myself if I knew we hadn't given you a chance to come back."

"When we attack," Wix warned the crowd, "the Arakkans will be crushed. We'll take you down, all of you." Maran saw by the cutting tone of his voice that Wix was as angry as ever. "Our army is stronger, we have five thousand men, many more men than you do, plus more experience. We'll beat you into the dirt."

The crowd responded sneeringly to the prisoner's brash predictions.

"What were you told?" Maran pleaded with Iri. "When you were drafted, what were you told? Did they mention that these people have been here long before the Frathi? Did they mention that they offered peace and the Frathi rejected it? Did they tell you they murdered a priest?"

"They told us that savages were discovered in the forest and that they had to be put down before they became a threat." Iri rubbed her grimy chin against her shoulder. "They said that bloodthirsty cannibals were plotting to come into Kalak Lar and Kalak Singh to kill us. Of course no one could let that happen. They were very convincing. There was a tremendous outcry."

"Enough!" the First shouted. "I have heard enough! You four, as representatives of your people and the Shlatlar, are guilty of the following crimes: The invasion of an Arakkan village; the brutal murder of a priest; the desecration of religious monuments; and attempted annihilation of an entire race. You will be sentenced to death. Execution by knife—your throats will be cut. Do you have any last words?"

"Maran, are you going to let him do this?" Iri's voice was shaking, frightened as she fought back tears.

I have never seen Iri cry before, Maran suddenly realized. She was always the strong one. Iri who never cried. Strong Iri who was going to excel in the police force. Beautiful Iri with large brown eyes and short dark hair. Iri who was as good as dead.

"Are you going to let them kill us? Maran?"

The question hung in the air. Maran stood impassively before them. Why wasn't she begging the First to let them live? she asked herself. Why wasn't she offering to take their place? She felt as though someone was controlling her. There could be only one explanation: she had changed. They weren't really her friends. Not anymore, anyway. They were part of a past that

no longer seemed relevant. They were Shlatlar. They wanted
to destroy her people. They were alien, unlike her. Maran's eyes
wandered and somehow she found herself looking at Alik. He
stared back at her, waiting, his face expressionless.

Alien, yes. And destroyers, maybe. Maran stared at the four
prisoners. *Could Alik be right, after all?*

"First, please . . . Let them go. They are just four in a big-
ger war. Surely their freedom won't make a difference." Maran
forced out the words. They seemed to not want to emerge from
her mouth.

The First turned his violet steel glare to her. Had he touched
upon a nerve? Uncovered a weakness in Maran? "Guards," he
muttered. And before Maran could speak again, two guards
gripped her arms.

"I can't stop him," Maran whispered. "I'm sorry. I can't
stop him." Alik looked away from her, turned, and disappeared
into the crowd. Maran squeezed her eyes closed, fighting back
tears. She heard the First order the prisoners taken into the field.

Maran heard her friends' cries, and steeled herself. They
were pleading with her to help save them. But she could not
help them. She had tried, and she had failed. That was the end
of it. The fact was, Maran wasn't the person they used to know;
she wasn't the person she used to know. And she could not go
back. The past was dead. Maran had to move forward. The
Arakkans needed her; she had to be strong. Maran turned from
the First and made her way through the crowd.

The water ran at an even pace, swirling gently around boulders
and shrubs that ventured out defiantly from the river bank. It
tugged at the leaves that dared come too close, wetting their
lips. The river gurgled to itself, a constant chatter amid the patient sighing of the wind in the trees. It had run like this for
many hundreds of years, and it would continue to do so, long
after there was no one left to sit on its shore, as Maran now did.

She perched atop one of the boulders that jutted out part-
way into the river. Below her, the water journeyed onward over
the pebble and stone riverbed. She could see the tiny rocks,

clearly one moment, then the next blurred by the current. "Clear then blurry, just like my life." Maran laughed a dry, humorless laugh. "Everything is changing so quickly. I am the one who is being whipped by the current, and not these stray leaves that float downstream. I'm the one who can't fight the current and go back to where I was. I wish I could." Her voice was a whisper as she talked to herself, trying to sort out her thoughts.

Maran tossed a pebble into the water, watched it sink to the bottom, ripples blooming out from the point of impact. She blinked and they were gone. Someday she would be gone too, the ripples she caused forgotten, swept away.

"And what would happen if I left now?" she mused to herself. "This morning I had been fully prepared to unite the Arakkans. My uniting speech was magnificent, and it served its purpose. The warriors under my command are so ready to work together, are ready for the battle. I was ready for the battle." She paused. "And then Iri and Wix and Daken and Rheet had to come. Now, I don't know what I'm doing! I was ready, and then when I was confronted with them, I cracked, I couldn't do what needed to be done! Why couldn't I have let them go? I'm such a fool, I'm such a . . . I betrayed them. I should have listened to Alik. I shouldn't have let myself be talked into this. But if my confidence falls, that will damage morale. I just can't let the warriors see it. I have to get out of here. I can't do this. I'm not a savior, I'm just a young girl trying to figure out my life, and I can't even figure that out. The last thing I want is this war. The last thing I need is this war. If I leave, Darryil can handle it. He's a good warrior, much better than I am. Or perhaps the attack will be called off. Maybe they would listen to Alik and try to find peace."

"Why didn't I listen to Alik?" she whispered. The image of his face masked in disappointment floated in her memory. *Yes. Peace is the answer.* But she couldn't stop now. She had crossed the point of no return when she allowed her friends to be led into the field.

"They were my friends. Why didn't I do something?" The question echoed around her. "Because I was afraid. I am carrying so much on my shoulders, and arguing too hard for their release would have undone everything. I hate myself for that."

Her whole world felt dark, black. Maran stared down at her reflection in the river and was surprised to see the face that looked back. It was her. For some reason, Maran had expected to see herself physically changed. But for the battle paint and feathers, she looked the same. Maran looked away in horror that she could have changed so radically inside, and not have had her physical appearance altered in the slightest. She wanted to look different, she wanted people to look at her and see the ugliness inside her soul so that she wouldn't be forced into the task of hiding it. So perhaps they would feel guilty for destroying her beauty and replacing it with foulness. But she was still beautiful. That much was still the same.

She looked up at the trees, swaying gently in the soft wind that stroked her hair. Maran could close her eyes and easily imagine that it was Aliksandar caressing her, and not the breeze. She missed his touch more than anything. Maran wished they could run away together and leave society behind. They would spend long hours talking and laughing like they used to, and they would paint. They would dance on the beach and take long moonlit walks. And at night they would curl up together on a bed of furs and fall asleep in each others' arms, in front of a blazing fire. Maran felt her heart begin to pound as she thought of the feel of his skin against hers, the gentle pressure of his strong arms around her body. She wanted to run back to him, not go forward in battle.

"But I can't go back. Not now."

Maran closed her eyes and tried to convince herself that she was doing the right thing. She was fighting for her home. For Aliksandar's home. She was fighting to protect the Arakkan children, to liberate them from the Shlatlar reign of terror. If her losing the man she loved meant that the Arakkans would survive, it was a small sacrifice. She had already lost him anyway. The chances of mending their love were so slim that they were nonexistent. He would never come back to her. Whatever she did wouldn't make that much difference. Maran had to save her people.

You may be Arakkan by blood, but you are Frathi in all other respects. Alik's words reverberated inside her head. "He was so right," she whispered. "My claim to being Arakkan is just that—a claim. I am a Frathi trapped in the body of an Arakkan. It was only by chance that I discovered Aliksandar's pod on the beach, not some prophetic workings. I . . . I am but a *convenience* for the First, little more than a figurehead for his campaign. He *used* me. The Frathi raised me, the Frathi educated me. The Arakkans gave me to the Frathi; I've been nothing but a symbol all along, something to be used—first, as a symbol of freedom; now, as a symbol of war. And Alik was the only one that had seen it." She laughed mirthlessly. "He alone had been able to see what had blinded me—the truth."

She closed her eyes, fighting back tears. "Alik and I—we're so much the same, but yet, so different, too . . ."

Maran looked back down at the river, her knees pulled up to her chest. "I have to go back. I must return to Kalak Lar one last time, to see my mother. Darryil can lead the army, I don't care. I have to know the truth, before the Frathi are beaten and my chance is lost."

Maran slid off the boulder and waded across the stream. The birds twittered overhead as she made her way through the forest to the Frathi city of Kalak Lar. It would be a long walk.

28

She had arrived during the night and was captured by one of the newly stationed guards at the perimeter of the city. Maran was unceremoniously shoved into the prison cell, an iron-barred door slamming shut behind her.

"The Master of the Council will see you at her convenience." The guard turned and left, his boot heels clacking down the tiled hallway.

Maran sat down on the rickety bunk and leaned against the stone wall. Though she had not been badly injured during her capture, her backside was sore. She had ended up going back to the village and taking a verhi, being sure to stay under cover. A furious gallop for most of the ride had shortened the trip by several hours, even though she had taken a different, longer route that would keep her away from any advancing troups.

But she was at least here now, she thought as she contemplated the dismal monotony of her cell. And she was going to see Jinas. That was what Maran had come to do. *That* was the only thing that mattered.

She closed her eyes and wondered if the attack had begun

yet. Somehow, she knew it had. Hopefully, Darryil had had enough time to fully prepare everyone. Hopefully, they were all cooperating, working together under Darryil's leadership. Maran knew he could do it; he was so much stronger than she. He knew things about battle that Maran could never even hope to learn in two lifetimes. She had faith that things would work. They had to work.

And what of Alik? Did he go to the caves with the other villagers? He must have. There was no place else for him to go and he certainly wasn't going to fight. She wondered if he would be looking for her when the army pulled out of Daar Nakl. Would he wonder why she wasn't there by Darryil's side, their leader, their prophecy come true? For some reason, Maran sensed he knew that she had come back to Kalak Lar. She sensed that he had known she would return even before Maran herself knew. Alik could predict her thoughts and actions. Alik knew Maran in ways she didn't imagine possible. And she had been so blind.

Footsteps clacked from down the hall, and though the walk sounded familiar, it was not Jinas' stride she heard. Frowning, Maran opened her eyes to see a man round the corner and stand on the other side of the prison bars.

It was Ranul.

He looked different in his military uniform. His blond hair was longer and pulled back in a short ponytail at the base of his neck. He seemed more muscular to Maran, and she decided that had been a result of his military training. But the greatest change was in his face. His eyes seemed to pierce her flesh from within their deepened sockets, his thin lips pursing slightly as he considered Maran.

"I heard that we had taken one of the savages prisoner, but I never expected to see you. Maran, you aren't one of them. You're Frathi."

"My blood is Arakkan," Maran said softly.

"Then you must have been part of some illicit affair between one of our people and one of the savages. You must have been adopted by Jinas. That's the only logical explanation for this."

"I was adopted, but that's not how it happened." Her voice

remained barely above a whisper. "This war is wrong, Ranul. The Frathi are the savages, not the Arakkans. We invaded their home, we killed their people. Why can't we just leave them alone?"

He stared at her, his blue eyes narrowing. "You've changed, Maran. I don't know you anymore. I don't know what happened, but you changed. There was a time when you would support the Frathi without question. What happened, Maran?"

Maran hesitated. "I met someone."

"Who?"

"A man. A man I love very much. One I hope still loves me."

Ranul shook his head. "Had you not changed, Maran, I would ask you to come back to me. I know we lost touch for a while, but you must believe that I thought of you every day and none of the women I was with were the same as you, Maran. You must believe me."

Maran remained silent. So, she thought, that was it. During the three years that she had remained loyal to his memory, *he* had found other women. No wonder he stopped writing.

Ranul sighed. "Well, Frathi or not, you have obviously made your choice. I want you to know that your turning to their side won't stop me from attacking the savages. In fact, the attack is already underway. The signal is long since given. By my estimates, half their troops should be finished by now, their village routed. Five thousand Frathi troops against any number would be fatal. Definitely routed." He turned to leave, shadows falling across his face. "Maran," he added, "we aren't taking any prisoners. I thought you should know." She didn't reply. Ranul shook his head and left.

Maran, where was Maran? Alik sat atop his nervous verhi, scanning the ranks for Maran's black hair, but if she was there, she blended in with everyone else.

"Do you see her?" Darryil shouted to him. Alik shook his head, urging his mount alongside Darryil's. "When did you see her last?" the warrior asked.

"Earlier, when the prisoners were taken to the fields, I saw her leave. But I didn't see where she went."

Darryil frowned, still searching for their leader. The villagers had made it to the caves, and now the warriors were in position to move out to the fields. But Maran wasn't present to lead them. Darryil fretted that the warriors' morale would be crushed without her there.

"Darryil," Alik shouted, "you have to lead them. We can't wait for Maran."

"I can't. I don't have the power she has over them."

Alik shook his head. "Yes, you do. Darryil, they'll follow you. Speak to them. Tell them what's happened."

Darryil frowned worriedly. "I don't know what to say. I can't explain where she is."

Alik reigned his nervous mount around. "Then I'll speak to them," he said, and rode off into the crowd. Darryil watched as Alik made his way to the center of the mass of warriors and somehow managed to focus their attention on him.

"Arakkan warriors, hear me! Listen to me! Maran has disappeared. We cannot find her. It seems that Tahar brought her to us just long enough to unite our forces. Now we must finish the job ourselves.

"And we can do it! Though there will be death on both sides, Maran . . ." He hesitated. "Maran was right. We have to stop the terror, the raids, and the torture. We must protect the future of our children. I'm not saying I was wrong, but I now see how she thought. And though I am not a warrior, I will ride with you, for I understand now that to do nothing, to say nothing, is to be nothing. I want us to win; that is why I now ride.

"That is also why I will follow Darryil, as you must follow him to ensure our success. His power as a warrior is great; he will lead you to victory if only you let him. He was there when Maran outlined the battle plans; he knows her thoughts and can execute them as well as she can. Granted, he was not part of the prophecy, but the prophecy only stated that we would be *led* to a new frontier. We have been led, my friends, and like children stepping away from their parents, it is time to take these final, crucial steps on our own. To be victorious as Arakkans, we must unite as pure Arakkans." He took a knife from his saddle pouch and raised it over his head. "Look to Darryil to unite us now!"

Moving as one, eighteen hundred heads turned to stare expectantly at Darryil. He in turn stared back at Alik, nodding slowly. "I will lead you!" he shouted, raising his fist into the air. "In the Spirit of Tahar, we ride against the Shlatlar now! Let us take position on the plains and wait for their folly!" The warriors roared in approval, battle cries rising into the air to be backed by eighteen hundred fists. Together, in a thundering mass, the warriors rode from the village, Alik among them.

Later that afternoon, Alik stared down from the hill and into the forest valley where the village rested. Clouds of smoke plumed and billowed, and Alik knew that the villagers' homes were gone. In his mind, he saw flames consume the bed where he had held Maran such a short time ago. He saw the fire eat away the walls and roof. Some of the paintings had been taken with the citizens, as had the records and the Umak's book of holy incantations. But once more, the Shlatlar had stripped Alik of all his worldly belongings.

He glanced over both shoulders at the Arakkan soldiers behind him, searching again for Maran.

Where could she be? What could have happened to her?

Tamald reined up between Alik and Darryil. "The Shlatlar troops that had attacked and burned the village are moving up the plain," he announced breathlessly. The Shlatlar soldiers were coming. They watched with knots in their throats as death slinked up the slope of the hill. One last time, Alik cast a searching glance over his shoulder.

Where is she?

Maran didn't know how long she had been sitting in the cell. It seemed like days. She could dimly hear shouting outside and wondered what was happening. Could they already have taken

Kalak Lar? If so, the battle was moving ahead of schedule. Maran wondered idly what Alik was doing, if he had accompanied the other villagers. And what would he do when the battle was over? What would she do? There wasn't a place for her in Arakkan society; her time as a figurehead would be over, and the Frathi certainly wouldn't want her back—nor would she go to them if they asked. Maran sighed and closed her eyes.

She heard footsteps in the hall again. It was Jinas, she knew. They came to a halt outside the door and Maran saw the woman standing before her, blond hair hanging in a long braid down the back of her starched white uniform. She looked older than Maran remembered, like she had aged twenty years in the few weeks Maran had been away.

"Maran."

Maran didn't immediately respond. She had come this far, but suddenly, she had no idea what to say. Her mind had simply gone blank.

"It's good to see you, though I'm sorry it had to be like this." Maran remained silent. Jinas continued. "I see you've discovered your true past. In a way, I'm glad, though I want you to know that I was going to tell you."

Maran studied Jinas quietly. "When?"

Jinas sighed. She unlocked the cell door and stepped inside, sitting down next to Maran on the cot. "Soon, very soon. I wasn't going to keep your past from you for much longer, even though the other council members thought I should. I just couldn't do that to you, Maran. We were going to tell the youth in 3392, on our fifty-year anniversary of settlement. Until then we were planning to just keep conditioning everyone."

"Brainwashing," Maran corrected.

"If you wish. But I thought you needed to know what happened, and now it looks like you do. Do you?"

Maran hesitated. "I know some of what happened. I know that the Frathi discovered Arakka and it was inhabited. I know that the Commander wanted power and waged war on the Arakkans. I was told that rulership changed hands several times between the peace factions and the war factions and that I was a symbolic gift to the Shlatlar—"

"Is that what they call us?" Jinas mused. "I had always wondered. Go on, Maran."

Maran hesitated again. "I know that the Shlatlar are in power now and they killed my parents. And that you adopted me when I was given to the Frathi."

"Actually," Jinas interrupted, "I'm not your original adoptive mother. She was killed and you were voted to me." She smiled sadly. "I never really wanted a child, but you haven't been too difficult."

Maran stared at Jinas. This woman hadn't wanted a child, but was saddled with one anyway. Maran's head was whirling. Everything was falling apart around her, and Maran could feel herself falling with it. Tears brimmed in her eyes. Jinas cast her glance downward.

"I'm sorry, Maran," she whispered.

"Why did you let me live? If the Shlatlar are in control, why was I allowed to live?"

This time it was Jinas who paused. "We feared an uprising from the Arakkans. If they saw their gift to us destroyed, they would undoubtedly lose control and attack. Even though we were and still are militarily more advanced than they are, we didn't want to take the chance. And no one was told of the Arakkans before now because of that very reason—we feared uprising and we couldn't have sympathy for them within our own people. Do you understand?"

Maran felt herself die inside just a little more. She wasn't kept alive because she was loved. She was kept alive as a convenience. Her whole life amounted to nothing more than a shaky treaty. Maran felt incredibly weak. *I wish Alik were here to hold me.* The thought flitted through her mind and she instantly banished it for its foolishness. Alik wasn't here. And if he were, he would only say that he had been correct, that he had told her but she had refused to see. Maran had to stand alone.

"Who told about the temple?" Maran asked softly.

"Iri did. But Maran, you mustn't be upset. She was worried when you didn't return from what she called 'a hike.' She told us where you had gone and how to get there; I sent a few troops to see that you were safe.

"We didn't expect to find the priest. I sincerely thought everyone at the temple had been killed ages ago. How he survived, we don't know. But we did what we had to do. Word would've made its way back to the city that he was there, and we couldn't let that stir up trouble. It was"—she turned both hands palm up—"necessary and expedient that he be killed. It was unfortunate, of course, Iri told us later that even she had no idea the priest was there. The troops went on to track you and found the village. We quickly realized that as soon as word of the priest's death reached the village, that there would be an uprising. So we commissioned a draft, because we knew there would be a war."

"Iri's dead."

Jinas sat in shocked silence. "What?"

Maran closed her eyes. "Iri's dead. Rheet's dead. Wix and Daken are dead. They were found coming to Daar Nakl from the temple. The First had them executed."

Jinas closed her eyes in silent prayer. She shook her head. "I never dreamed it would come out this way. Never in my wildest imaginings." Maran didn't respond. Jinas sighed. "Our main arm of forces attacked the village yesterday. Ranul was with them. Last I heard, the battle was very heated. Maran, when they return, they won't want you spared. You'll be killed as an enemy prisoner. Despite everything, I am not completely without maternal feelings, Maran. I hate to think what they would do to you." She paused. "I'm letting you go. If you can find your way out of Kalak Lar, you'll be safe."

Maran stared at Jinas, letting the woman's words sink into her mind. Her world was still a haze and she wasn't quite sure she had heard Jinas correctly. The idea of being released, Maran had never thought possible. She had expected to be killed. Now, she was being let go.

Slowly, Maran rose to her feet. Jinas did not stand with her and made no move to stop Maran. A silent moment passed between them, a moment of final understanding, and words that were too much to be said drifted in the quiet space, unheard. Maran nodded, turned, and strode out of the cell, leaving Jinas—and her past—behind.

29

The pistol lay in her lap, smooth, sleek, beautiful. She admired the way the dim light reflected off its silver barrel, the contours of its black handle. Her fingers traced along its edges, feeling the cool hardness beneath their tips. It was a shame something so lovely had to be so deadly.

They were losing. She hadn't had the heart to admit it. A chance remained that the soldiers could regroup and mount a new offensive. But they didn't have enough time. The enemy was moving much too swiftly. Their power had been drastically underestimated. Defeat now seemed inevitable. As had victory, only a short time ago.

She pointed the pistol upward, staring down into the barrel's darkness. *Oblivion,* she thought to herself. Her life would not be spared, she knew. Most likely she would be tortured until she died. She couldn't face that; it was too horrible to even consider. This was the only way, the only alternative.

Jinas tightened her finger around the trigger. There was a click, then darkness as she slumped to the floor.

*   *   *

Smoke and fire were thick on the streets as Maran made her way down the once pleasant avenues of Kalak Lar. All around her houses, trees, and buildings burned, red tongues licking at the air, slurping up oxygen on which to feed. Great black clouds of smoke billowed from ruined roofs, blotting out the sun, and everywhere battle cries echoed and twined with the screams of the dying. Maran saw glimpses of troops running between places of cover and of warriors on verhi, their hair tied with blood-colored feathers and flying out around their heads, their bodies silhouetted against the violent backdrop.

Maran herself stayed close to the trees and shrubs that grew along the sidewalk and up to the trashed houses, giving herself cover should she need it. Once or twice she stumbled, almost falling over a body in her path, the fighter's eyes wide and unseeing in death. More often than not, the soldier was Frathi.

She heard a blast of gunfire and took shelter in a crumbling, burned-out building. Most of the roof was missing and Maran crouched in a corner near the edge of a gaping hole that had been knocked in the brick wall. From her vantage point she watched as a group of mounted Arakkan warriors using only knives and crossbows quickly took out a squadron of Frathi troops. Maran was greatly impressed; the warriors worked well together, keeping their mounts always moving in a swinging circular motion to provide a difficult target. Only one Arakkan was felled in contrast to over half of the Shlatlar fighters. The others retreated in haste, fleeing backward so as to not be vulnerable. But it was no use; three more were taken out even as they backed away.

A thundering boom sounded nearby and Maran felt the ground beneath her shake. Rubble fell, cascading from the sides of the building in which she hid and pelted all around her. Maran looked up in time to see a piece rain down on her, striking her on the head and knocking her unconscious.

*   *   *

When Maran regained her senses, there was silence. All around her was the acrid smell of smoke, and death seemed to hang in the air. She rubbed her head where the brick had struck her and found a large knot beneath her palm. She groaned and stood up, stepping over the foundation and out onto the charred remnants of lawn. From her new position, she surveyed her surroundings.

The scene around her was one of utter destruction. The Frathi city had almost been burned to the ground; only a few buildings remained standing. Smoke still wisped from blackened surfaces and warriors rode in and out of it on their way to various duties. None of them seemed to notice Maran as she stepped out into the street and began walking along the main road. Several times Maran thought she saw Darryil or Diella, but upon closer inspection, she saw that she was mistaken.

"Maran! Maran!" She spun around to see a young warrior striding up to her, his hand raised to signal her. It was Tamald. A surge of relief ran through Maran's body as he reached her side. She became weak in the knees and collapsed into him; he held her firmly as she leaned against his chest, trying to draw from his strength. A week ago he would have been excited at the prospect of holding her this closely; now his only concern was her health and stability.

"Are you all right?" he asked, peering down into her face. "You've got a nasty bump on your head."

Maran merely nodded even though her head throbbed. "I'm fine."

"We won," Tamald stated. "Your plans—taking the Shlatlar from the plains and using fire logs and double envelopment—it worked. We drove them against the lake and crushed them, then came to the cities and finished the job. We used fire as our main weapon. And you were right that they lost a lot of troops in the forest, to the bog and swamps. I suppose I never realized how dangerous it really was. We Arakkans are just used to it. But they weren't and that worked to our advantage. We couldn't have done it without your help, Maran."

Maran smiled faintly. "Where are the others, Darryil and Diella, the First and the Umak?"

"The Umak went with the villagers to the caves. The First was killed and Diella was wounded, though not badly—just a shoulder injury. She should be fine. Darryil was almost killed, but his life was saved by the knife of a valiant fighter who slit the Shaltlar's throat right open, just as Darryil was about to get it between the eyes. It was a good save."

"Who was it?" Maran asked, taking Tamald's arm as they walked to one of the few remaining buildings.

"Alik."

Maran froze. "What?"

Tamald grinned. "Alik. At the last minute, when you were nowhere to be seen, Alik convinced the people that they should follow Darryil and not wait for you. He said that you were right and we have to protect our future. Alik rode into battle with us and ended up saving Darryil's life. Darryil is with Prestun now, probably at this moment discussing his brush with death."

Maran's mouth hung open in shock. "Alik?" she repeated. "Alik went into battle? Where is he now?"

Tamald shrugged. "We don't know. Several people thought they had seen him but he's disappeared. We need to find him. The remaining Frathi, the women, children, and remaining soldiers were taken to Kalak Singh to a containment facility. They inform us that they're ready to talk peace. Alik is the only person that truly remembers the Old Times when there was peace. We feel he's the most well versed on the subject; we thought we'd let him do the talking. It's just that we can't find him."

Maran was thoughtful for a moment. "I think I know where he is, Tamald." She took her arm from his supportive shoulder and smiled at him. "Tell Darryil I'm going to find Alik."

"How do you know where he is?" Tamald was confused, and it was evidenced by his furrowed brow.

"I just have a hunch," Maran replied. "I'll see you later." She increased her pace to a jog and found the main road. She passed skeletal trees, licked clean by tongues of flame. The once beautiful lawns were crisp and black, white smoke rising from them. Across an expanse of rubble foundations, Maran spied the lot where her home once stood; its walls were crumbled, furniture blackened and strewn through the street. One of her half-finished paintings hung from a tree, like a ghostly effigy. Maran shook her head, pulling down her ponytail and letting her hair loose around her shoulders. The wind whispered around her as she followed the road out of Kalak Lar.

30

Maran pulled off her riding boots, tossing them into the pale grass, and scampered down the slope, feeling the sand slide beneath her bare feet. She removed the leather armor that covered her vest and thighs. None of it was necessary now. She dropped the pieces in the sand as she continued her brisk stride to the placid shoreline. She stopped several feet from the water's edge and sat down in the sand, next to Aliksandar's quiet, brooding form, crossing her legs as he had.

The two sat together in silence for several minutes. Maran wondered what he was thinking. It was strange seeing him here, where they had met not so many weeks ago; here, where she had opened the pod and seen his handsome face, where she had fallen in love with him before even knowing his name. Not far away was the cave where they had picnicked and danced, where he had first kissed her. She closed her eyes, letting the memories play out in her head and fade to darkness.

"We won." Aliksandar's voice was soft, barely above a whisper. It was a monotone statement, holding no emotion at all. His voice was blank, as was his face.

Maran nodded, opening her eyes again and looking out over the gentle ripples in the water. "I know. I spoke with Tamald."

Alik pulled his knees up to his chest and wrapped his arms around them. It was as if he were holding himself together. He looked thoughtful; Maran did her best not to seem like she was pressuring him.

"Did he tell you what happened?"

Maran nodded again, slowly. "He told me you fought. That you saved Darryil's life." She paused, waiting for him to speak, but he didn't. She continued. "Why, Alik? When you were so against the war, why did you fight?"

Alik was quiet for a long few minutes. She could practically hear him thinking. When he spoke, his voice was very quiet. "Because you were right. We have to protect our future at all costs. I knew that you were convinced it was the right thing to do; I knew that the Frathi would not want to talk peace. And I knew that in order to love you, I had to be able to try to understand how you thought. That's why I fought, because I loved you and I wanted you to know that I supported you. And because I had to listen to my own words. I don't believe in violence or hate, but I do believe in compromise, and I knew I had to compromise. With you, if no one else."

He paused, gathering his thoughts into words. "When I saved Darryil, I knew that I had done the right thing. They fight differently from us; they have no honor, no sense of dignity. When one of our men would fall, the Frathi riders would not even try to avoid trampling the body. They didn't care if our dead were desecrated. Winning was all that mattered to them. Rules didn't matter, only victory.

"And killing that commander, cutting his throat—it was wrong, but it was right. He fell in a puddle of mud near the lake shore. His starched white uniform was soiled, his blond hair streaked with mud. And I sat there on my verhi, just staring at him as the blood pulsed from his throat and he made faint strangling noises. He was trying to call out for help, staring straight up at me, begging me to help him. But I didn't. I found myself wondering if I had done the correct thing. It disgusted me that I could do something like that, but it sickened me more thinking of Darryil being killed." Alik hesitated, dropping his voice even lower. "But I don't regret doing it."

Maran listened to him, silently. When he described the commander, his blond hair and white uniform, Maran knew instantly that it had been Ranul. Strangely, she felt nothing. No remorse, no emptiness at his loss. Maran realized suddenly that to her, Ranul had died years ago, when she lost touch with him. It had been foolish of her to try to keep his memory alive.

But for some reason, Maran was saddened by the change in Alik. She hadn't wanted Darryil to be killed any more than Alik did, but he had lost his innocence in saving the warrior's life. No longer could he claim to be a complete pacifist; he had killed.

"Alik," Maran said softly, "I didn't fight."

He looked abruptly at her, brow furrowed. "I knew you didn't lead, but I thought you would catch up later. Then when I didn't see you after the battle, I thought you were in Kalak Singh. But you didn't fight at all?"

Maran shook her head, feeling ashamed. "I fulfilled my part of the prophecy: I brought the Arakkans together. It never said that I had to lead you into battle. That was something created by the First." She paused, staring down at her hands. "But that's not the only reason I didn't fight. You were right, Alik. I am more Frathi than Arakkan. I was foolish to try to instantly fit in to Arakkan society and just shelve the Frathi heritage I had known all my life. I couldn't fight them not knowing my full story, my history. I had to go back and speak with Jinas, to find out the things that the First hadn't been able to tell me. I had to know the whole truth."

"And did you find out what you wanted to know?" Alik asked the question gently.

Maran hesitated for a moment. "Yes, yes I did. I know it all now, and I'm glad. I finally feel like I can start over again. I want to make a new life for myself." Maran paused. "What about you?"

Alik frowned. "I've seen both sides, the good and the evil.

I've preached peace and now I've killed. I've done both. I know what it's like now." He shook his head in bewilderment. "I know what it's like."

"Tamald said they want you to govern them," Maran said. "They want you to head the new government. He said they feel that since you were on a government council before the Pod Mission, then you are the most experienced in peace. Even though you killed a man, they want you to lead them. Are you going to do it?"

"I feel it's ironic, but I suppose I must. I almost feel like I'm cheating them; I'm not a purist anymore. When I heard, I almost said that they had the wrong man; I wonder if there is someone better. But I will, if they want, only because I believe in the future, that we can live in a peaceful world. Maybe not truly in my lifetime, but in the children's, I feel sure. We can have peace, and I . . . I'm going to try.

"But I can't do it alone. I'll need someone to help me, someone to govern with me." He paused. "Maran, I'd like that to be you."

Maran was silent. A cold hardness settled in her chest and she was suddenly angry. "All my life I have been a symbol. I was a gift of peace, I was a shaky treaty, I was a figurehead for the First's war. I will not be your symbol, Alik. I won't rule with you just because I'm Frathi *and* Arakkan, just because I symbolize the unity you want. I won't be used anymore. I'm my own person and I'm going to take my own path, not follow your whim."

Alik shook his head, startled at her reaction. "Maran, I don't want you with me for any of that. I want you . . . as my wife. Because I love you. I love you, Maran." He took her hands in his own. "The pain of being without you is something I never want to live through again. I was wrong to expect you to always see things my way. I'll never do that again. But I was so ashamed of the way I had treated you that I couldn't ask you . . . I didn't know how . . . I couldn't . . ." He sighed. "I was wrong about not being able to love you when you believed like you did. What you were doing was for all of us. For your home as well as mine. It was for us all, and when I realized that, I knew that helping in the effort was the only answer. I wanted to support you because I love you.

"Maran"—he leaned toward her—"forgive me for hurting you as I did." He stared into Maran's deep violet eyes, seeing tears peek from their corners and trickle down her cheeks. Slowly, he raised his hand and gently brushed them away with his fingertips.

"Alik," Maran whispered, her hand caressing his cheek, "I wanted it to be so perfect. But everything seemed to go so wrong. I knew for certain that you didn't love me; I thought you hated me, in fact. I thought I had lost you and that it wouldn't matter if I led the war because you didn't want me anymore. I thought that you were ashamed of me."

"I was ashamed of myself."

Maran shook her head sadly. "When you asked me *ambrie*, it was the happiest moment of my life. I want us to have that happiness again." Alik drew her into his arms and held her tightly. But he did no more. He buried his face in the crook of her neck and held her as their emotions came flooding out and they cried in each other's arms. The two shook with sobs, their shame and frustration draining out of them. Maran let all of her confusion and hate pour out, let it be washed away down her face. Alik felt his depression and restlessness begin to subside and fade away as he discovered that his true place was here in Maran's arms. It had been all along.

"Maran," he said softly, drawing back from her, "I want to show you my mindvoice. Don't be frightened, it won't hurt. But it's something I should have done long ago. Will you let me?"

Maran nodded. Alik lay his hands on Maran's temples, his palms against her ears. She instantly placed her hands on him in the same fashion, letting her eyes flutter close as he closed his.

Colors began to bloom and flower in Maran's head, first as gentle pastels—pinks, pale blues, and light yellows—then growing to vibrant reds, royal blues, and flashing yellows. The hues and shades exploded, and with the explosions flooded an all-consuming, powerful force of love that Maran had never experienced the like of before in her life. Her mind staggered at its intensity, but then surged forward, reciprocating equally with her own love, showering it in Aliksandar's head like a thousand glorious fireworks.

Maran saw Alik in her mind's landscape and suddenly she was there with him, standing in the center of the rainbow of bright explosions, enveloped in his arms. She was consumed by love for him; all Maran wanted to do was stay in his strong, gentle arms.

Somehow, in her mind, Maran found that her consciousness was watching herself and Alik. She could see his arms tighten around her as the colors swirled all about them in the surreal landscape of their minds. A coil of violet and lavender wrapped itself around them, spinning round and round and raising a breeze that stroked at their hair and skin, whipping gently at their clothes. Her consciousness circled their bodies slowly, observing from all angles how they held each other close, the colors around them rainbowed and burst even more wildly, creating a blur of tints and hues. Maran felt swollen with ecstasy, with the joy of Aliksandar's love, at feeling him so closely against her and hearing the colorful song of his mind-voice. And he was reveling in bliss at hearing hers.

Alik drew his hands away from her and the images faded and disappeared. She was left staring into his eyes, dazed at the power of his love for her, awed at her own love for him. He cared for her, an unbelievable caring that had no true words, only images. Had she not seen it, Maran would never have thought its strength possible.

"Maran," Alik whispered. "Will you be my wife and my partner?"

Maran nodded, still a bit dazed. "Alik, nothing in life would make me happier than spending the rest of it with you. I would be honored to be your wife."

A wide smile crossed Aliksandar's face and he took Maran into his arms, holding her tightly. She lay her head on his shoulder and smiled to herself.

Alik knew the Artisan Superior had been correct. Once his spirit was settled, his restlessness gone, he would find himself.

And he had. Never again would he let his love with Maran be broken. She was too valuable to him to ever lose.

Maran was content. Finally, her demons were at peace. She knew who she was; she knew what she was. No longer did she need to lie awake at night, confused and frustrated because she felt out of place among her own people. She had no true people, but it didn't matter now. Their whole society was going to be reconstructed; Maran could make a new start there with Alik. She would be his wife, his queen. She would be his friend, his confidante, his lover. Nothing could take her away from him.

Maran smiled again as the gentle sea breeze caressed their skin. She was at peace, finally.

I have come home.